THE PLEASURE OF A PIRATE

LINDA RAE SANDE

The Pleasure of a Pirate

V1

Cover photograph © Period Images.com

Cover art by Twisted Teacup Publishing

All rights reserved - used with permission.

Edited by Katrina Teele-Fair

http://www.lindaraesande.com

ISBN: 978-1-946271-43-3

Twisted Teacup Publishing, Cody, Wyoming

The Secrets of a Viscount

The Widowers of the Aristocracy

The Dream of a Duchess

The Vision of a Viscountess

The Conundrum of a Clerk

The Charity of a Viscount

The Cousins of the Aristocracy

The Promise of a Gentleman

The Pride of a Gentleman

The Holidays of the Aristocracy

The Christmas of a Countess

The Knot of a Knight

The Heirs of the Aristocracy

The Angel of an Astronomer

The Puzzle of a Bastard

The Choice of a Cavalier

The Bargain of a Baroness

The Jewel of an Earl's Heir

The Vixen of a Viscount

Stella of Akrotiri

Origins

Deminon

Diana

CHAPTER 1

A MASKED BALL

ord Weatherstone's mansion, Mayfair, 1819

Doing his best not to gawk at those who made up the crush of Lord Weatherstone's masked ball, Blake Russell stood near the refreshment table and drank a glass of champagne. Not used to the fizzy drink, he was pondering how he might surreptitiously replace it with brandy when the orchestra launched into the second dance set of the night.

He glanced around, wondering if he should ask one of the young women to dance. There were a half-dozen of them lined up along one wall, all dressed in gowns of white and wearing masks that barely covered their faces.

All except for one young lady.

She wore a gilded mask that covered all but her bright red lips and square chin. Brown hair, piled high atop her head in a riot of curls, seemed dusted with glitter, for it shined bright under the ballroom's candlelight. Her gown, a pink frock topped with a white pinafore, suggested she had raided her lady's maid's grandmother's trunk in an effort to look like Little Bo Peep.

Although the gown was doing its best to contain her generous bosom and excelled at highlighting her slim waist, Blake thought her feminine charms would topple out should she lean forward too much. As for her hips, there was really no way to know if they were wide or not since the sides of her gown were supported by small panniers.

Or perhaps those *were* her hips, and she really did have a figure best likened to that of an hourglass.

Blake felt a stirring in his groin at the thought of bedding such a creature, and he groaned in despair. He had been far too long without a woman, and with his ship due to sail on the morrow, this ball would be his last entertainment for at least a month.

And his last land-based assignment for the Foreign Office before he resumed his regular posting.

Locate Lord Dorchester and watch his every move. Report in the morning before the Molly sets sail.

When Blake had agreed to take over the captaincy of the *Molly*, he had done so knowing he would have to pretend to be a pirate on occasion. He didn't know he might have to take on other guises when he was on dry land.

If this hadn't been a masked ball, Blake knew someone else would have had this assignment. He couldn't pass for a member of the peerage—or even a gentleman, for that matter—if he wasn't wearing a mask and the clothes he wore when he was playing a pirate.

He had almost argued with Lord Chamberlain when he was given the assignment. The head of the Foreign Office, the viscount seemed to think it a lark that Blake was still in London and could see to this quick assignment.

Attend for the experience, Lord Chamberlain had said. *If you don't know anyone, just watch from the side-lines and take note on how everyone else behaves. If you spot Dorchester, stay close. He's spread some vowels about town, his barony is broke, and there's talk he may attempt a robbery and fence the goods or perhaps leave the country with them. If he does the latter, you will have to go after him.*

At first, Blake had thought it unlikely anyone would attempt to knick something of value during a ball. Now that he'd had a chance to study the layout of Lord Weatherstone's mansion, he understood how it could be done.

Weatherstone's library was filled with small treasures from his travels. The desk in the study featured a solid gold quill pen. Lady Weatherstone's jewel box was in plain sight atop her dressing table. The parlor was decorated with all manner of expensive trinkets.

There were larger artifacts, of course, but it was unlikely the baron would attempt to lift a caryatid or the jewel-encrusted globe from the library.

Figuring out which gentleman was Dorchester was easy—the butler had announced him upon his arrival in the ballroom. Although the man had come in with a mask in hand, he hadn't put it on until the first dance was well underway.

Blake guessed the baron would have a dance partner for the second set, but Dorchester instead seemed to confer with a number of gentlemen before wandering off toward the supper room.

Following at a safe distance, Blake made sure to head straight for the tray of lobster patties once he was in the opulent room. If the baron was truly in dire straights as to his purse, it was likely he would opt for the more expensive foods at the other end of the table. He'd probably been living on the same fare as his servants, which meant crustaceans for most meals.

Downing part of his lobster patty, Blake dared a glance in the baron's direction, noting how the man was filling a plate with ham, roast beef and lamb.

Supposition confirmed.

Now he just had to keep an eye on the baron until the end of the ball. Which turned out to be easy.

Until it wasn't.

Dorchester finished his meal and returned to the ballroom, which had grown far more crowded. Blake lost sight of the baron several times, but when he confirmed the man was dancing with one of the white-gowned young ladies, he made his way to the buxom Little Bo Peep he had noticed earlier.

"We seem to be the only ones in costumes from the prior century," he remarked.

Behind the mask, the girl's eyes widened. "We are?" she asked as she looked to her left and right, as if she thought he might have directed his query to someone else.

"Aye, milady," he replied, using his best pirate voice. "Blake's my name, and pirating is my game. And who might you be?" He knew it was entirely inappropriate to introduce himself to a young lady, but there was no one around to do the honors. Apparently, her chaperone was dancing.

A giggle escaped the young woman before she said, "Barbara. Miss Barbara Wycliff," she said, emphasizing the 'Miss'. "But for tonight, I am Bo Beep."

Blake blinked. He had guessed correctly as to her costume. He glanced around. "You seem to have lost your sheep," he replied.

"Indeed. And my lady's maid. She's already been asked to dance."

"Then may I have this dance?"

The bright red lips split into a huge smile. "Yes, yes of course," she gushed. She placed her hand on his proffered arm and allowed him to lead her to where couples were lining up for an English country dance. They had barely taken their places when the orchestra played the opening strains, and they were off and performing the spirited dance.

From his perspective in the line, Blake was able to keep an eye on Dorchester, who was just a few men down the line from him.

When his partner was within hearing range, he asked, "Which one is your lady's maid?" The comment about her lady's maid hadn't seemed odd when she first mentioned it—the maid was no doubt acting as her chaperone—but now that he had noticed all those on the dance floor were young, he had his doubts.

"Third one down on the right," Barbara replied. "Dancing with the tall gentleman," she added, obviously admiring the man Blake knew to be Lord Dorchester. "I wouldn't have invited her to attend with me, but it is a masked ball, and who would know she's a maid?" she commented.

Blake was about to admit he wasn't a member of the peerage, but thought better of it. The name 'Wycliff' had just made its way to his addled brain. "I should think the daughter of Sir Peter Wycliff would be allowed any companion she wished for this ball," he replied, hoping he had guessed correctly.

Barbara's eyes widened behind the mask. "So you won't tell anyone? About my lady's maid, I mean?"

Blake blinked behind his own mask. "I'm a pirate. I shan't tell a soul."

She grinned and was on to the next partner before she could respond. When they were once again paired, she asked, "Where do you live, Mr. Blake?"

He was tempted to mention Picadilly—he kept an apartment there for the periods of leave he was in London—but instead he said, "On my ship. The *Molly*."

She giggled again, the musical sound causing an unusual reaction in his nether region.

What was it about Miss Barbara Wycliff that had his body behaving as if she were some doxy he had hired for the night? She was a lady! A miss, really, since her father wasn't a member of Parliament. He was only a commoner, as was she.

But he was wealthy.

"You think I'm jesting?" he teased. "Where do *you* live?"

Barbara had to delay her response when she was sent whirling from his hold to the man next to him. When they finally rejoined in the dance, she said, "Mayfair. Here in Park Lane."

Blake nodded his understanding. She was the daughter of a baronet. Entirely out of his league. Which he would have been glad to accept, except...

He wasn't.

When the dance came to an end, and she was once again facing him, he leaned down. His lips covered hers in a quick kiss before they moved lower and kissed the back of her silk-gloved hand.

Entirely inappropriate. Very scandalous. Unforgivable.

Except no one seemed to notice but her.

She was staring up at him with the oddest expression before she was whisked away by another gentleman for the next dance.

Blake stood staring at where she'd been standing

for several seconds, his attempt to get his body under control failing miserably.

What the hell had just happened?

He glanced around, sure Sir Peter was about to pummel him into the dance floor. He'd just kissed the baronet's daughter in front of everyone at a *ton* ball.

But no one seemed to have noticed.

Couples were lining up for the next dance, though, acting as if he wasn't even there.

Blake wandered in a daze until he was in the area where the wallflowers were gathered. A few dared glances in his direction, as if they hoped he might honor them with a dance.

He was just about to oblige one of them when he remembered the reason he was there.

Dorchester.

He cursed under his breath, and his gaze scanned the dance floor. When he didn't spot Dorchester among those performing the spirited Scottish reel, he headed out the nearest ballroom door and hurried through the wide halls, glancing left and right in the event the baron might have ducked into a nearby room.

When Blake didn't find him in the library or the study—he had to apologize profusely for having interrupted a liaison between the Marquess and

Marchioness of Morganfield—he returned to the ballroom.

Thinking perhaps Dorchester might be in the gardens, he made his way to the back of the ballroom and out the French doors. From the flags leading to the famous Weatherstone gardens, Blake searched for the baron. Given the number of couples engaged in all manner of naughty behavior—and the number of alcoves in the hedges in which they could engage in naughty behavior—it took him some time to determine that Lord Dorchester was not among them.

He felt relief when he realized Little Bo Peep wasn't, either.

Back in the ballroom, he heaved a sigh of relief at finding Little Bo Beep dancing.

He groaned when he saw it was with Lord Dorchester.

How had he lost track of them?

Watching from the sidelines, he wondered at his reaction. What was it about Miss Barbara Wycliff that had him feeling so possessive? As if he had been the first one to find her, so he thought only he should be entitled to dance with her? To covet her? To expect that he would be the only one allowed to kiss her?

"Thank the gods a waltz is next," a gentleman to his right said, although not necessarily to Blake.

"Followed by a trip to the supper room," a man

wearing a jester's hat and mask said to his left. "Lord Weatherstone's spreads are always the best."

"Agreed. In fact, I may skip the waltz and go eat," the first man said.

Blake blinked as both men left his company and headed for the supper room.

When the dance set ended and Bo Beep bowed to Lord Dorchester, Blake moved in and lifted her hand to his arm.

"Blake!" she said with a huge smile.

The baron's brows furrowed, but he made no complaint and instead stepped back. "I will come for you at two o'clock in the afternoon, my lady," he said before bowing and then giving Blake a dagger-filled look.

Blake ignored the baron's expression and turned his attention on Barbara. "Will you waltz with me?"

Her eyes widened behind the mask. "I've never danced a waltz," she said with a shake of her head.

Determined to have her company for the next half-hour, Blake allowed a shrug. "It's an easy dance to learn. I will teach you," he said, just as the opening strains of the dance began. "Follow my lead."

Barbara gave him an uncertain glance but did as she was told, placing a white-gloved hand on his shoulder and allowing him to support her other with his upraised hand. A few steps into the dance, and she was soon performing the simple routine.

"You're doing wonderfully," he said as he led them into the circle of other dancers.

"Only because you're such a strong lead," she argued.

"Your costume is perfection. Even without the sheep."

"I almost brought my sheepdog, but I didn't think he would do well in such a crush," she replied. "Lord Weatherstone might have banished him to the gardens."

Blake grinned. "He would have us all herded onto the dance floor." He glanced around, realizing nearly everyone was dancing. "Much like this waltz seems to have done." Upon his next turn, though, he noticed Dorchester glaring at him from where he stood against a wall. "How well do you know Lord Dorchester?"

Barbara seemed to have difficulty with her next few steps before she recovered. "I do not. At least, I had not met him before this evening," she amended.

Frowning, Blake dared another glance in the baron's direction. "And yet he is coming for you at two o'clock?" he countered.

"For a ride in the park, yes," Barbara acknowledged. "I receive so few offers, I feel as if

I really must accept every one that comes my way."

Blake nearly lost his place in the dance. "Surely you jest," he countered. "And if you do not—"

"I do not."

"—Then please reconsider his invitation. He is under investigation by the very highest of authorities here in England," Blake said in a hoarse whisper. "Your virtue could be at risk."

He watched as her eyes widened behind the mask, almost as if she wanted her virtue to be at risk.

Damnation!

"Surely he cannot be all bad," she replied, her manner suggesting she thought Blake was teasing her.

Blake dared another glance in Lord Dorchester's direction. "Perhaps not all," he agreed, noting how the wallflowers had begun fluttering their fans in the baron's direction. Dorchester looked miserable.

Finding he couldn't feel the least bit sorry for Dorchester, though, Blake turned his attention back on his dance partner. "Are you enjoying the evening?"

She nodded. "I am, thanks to you," she replied as her gaze settled on her lady's maid. The young woman was engaged in a rather spirited conversation with Lord Dorchester, almost as if she were scolding the baron. "And you?"

Blake allowed a huge smile. "Likewise. Perhaps

you'll allow me to escort you to the supper when this dance has ended?"

Barbara's face seemed to fall. "I have already told Lord Dorchester he may have that honor," she said in a most apologetic tone. "Perhaps at the next ball?"

Trying hard to hide his disappointment, Blake finally gave a shake of his head. "I must depart for the Channel in the morning," he replied. "A matter of national security."

Her eyes once again widening behind the mask, Barbara was about to ask for more information when the music ended and Lord Dorchester appeared at her elbow.

"My lady?" he said before he whisked her off in the direction of the supper room, not giving Blake a chance to even bow to Little Bo Peep.

Blake bristled at losing his grip on the baronet's daughter. She had been so easy to speak with. So easy to dance with. He had already decided she probably wasn't easy on the eyes—otherwise, why would she have worn a mask that nearly covered her entire face? —but her delectable body and engaging company more than made up for any deficiencies she might have in appearance.

Watching as Lord Dorchester led the lust of his life into the supper room, Blake took up a position just outside the arched doorway, determined to intercept Bo Peep when she moved to leave. Perhaps he could secure permission to send a letter whilst on his next mission.

Permission to pay a call on her when he returned to London.

Whenever the *Molly* returned to Wapping, which wouldn't be until his crew had located and arrested the French privateer who was apparently flooding Suffolk with illegal brandy wine.

Blake hung around the refreshment table for a time, his gaze trained on the entrance to the supper room. He spotted a number of familiar aristocrats helping themselves to the aspic and Yorkshire pudding, to the strawberries and sliced beef. Although his stomach grumbled, he resisted the urge to join them lest he miss Barbara taking her leave of the supper room.

When the orchestra played the opening strains of the next dance, several couples emerged from the supper room followed by a tidal wave of aristocrats.

At no point did he see Barbara. Nor did he see Lord Dorchester or even Barbara's lady's maid leave the supper room.

Sure the room was nearly empty, Blake made his way in and searched in vain. No Barbara. No Dorchester. No lady's maid.

He frowned, noting there were two other exits out

of the supper room, although both led to the same hallway. He glanced up and down the hall, a hint of panic gripping him when he didn't spy his prey strolling the Aubusson carpet lining the hall.

Thinking Little Bo Peep might have gone to the gardens for air, he went back out and discovered a similar situation to what he had seen earlier—but no Barbara. No Dorchester.

Back in the ballroom, his gaze scanned the crowd.

His search for Barbara Wycliff proved futile.

Even her lady's maid was no longer in the ballroom.

The retiring room, perhaps?

Daring a glance in and hearing only gasps of protest, he quickly closed the door and heaved a sigh of frustration.

Even Dorchester seemed to have gone missing.

Disgusted by his failure to keep tabs on his Bo Peep and Lord Dorchester, Blake took his leave of Lord Weatherstone's mansion.

Just in time to see Lord Dorchester's coach pull away from the curb and head out at a rather unsafe speed. A second later, and Sir Peter Wycliff's town coach followed.

What the hell?

Hailing a hackney proved easier than he expected, but given the other coaches' head starts, Blake's driver was unable to determine the direction they might have taken once they had reached Oxford Street.

Angry at himself for having lost his prey—and Little Bo Peep—Blake had the driver take him to Wapping and the wharf closest to where his ship was docked.

He had a letter to write to Lord Chamberlain.

CHAPTER 2

AN UNEXPECTED ASSIGNMENT

he following morning
"Did you wear the cutlass to the ball last night?" Nelson asked as he gave the captain a cursory glance. From the moment Blake Russell had told him he was attending a costume ball, the first mate thought to tease him. "Surprised the butler would have let you into his mansion."

Blake lifted the curved sword to one side, pretending he intended to bring it down on Nelson's green skull-capped head. "Not only did I wear it, but I'm glad I did. A young lady dressed as Little Bo Beep agreed to dance wth me."

Nelson's bushy eyebrows waggled. "What did she do with her sheep while she danced with you?"

"Left 'em in the gardens," Blake replied, playing along with his first mate's teasing. He sobered and struck a pose meant to strike fear in the hearts of anyone who dare board his ship—or take command of it.

The first mate cocked an eyebrow. "Ye certainly look like a swarthy pirate. Are you thinking to behead someone?"

Blake gave Nelson a quelling glance. Given his dark hair, broad chest, beefy hands, and the permanent tan he had acquired whilst at sea, Blake had the 'swarthy' in spades. And the seadog had over two decades of experience as a crewman. "I was hoping to strike a bit of fear into the miscreant who thinks to take command of my ship," he replied. "I cannot believe Fitz challenged me last night when I boarded." He pulled on his black leather vest, and then considered donning the gold rings and chains that helped to complete his ensemble as the captain of a pirate ship. They had certainly worked well at the Weatherstone ball.

Nelson rolled his own eyes. "Fitz was three sheets to the wind, I tell you. He won't even remember he challenged you. And just why the hell would you attend a costume ball?"

Blake rolled his eyes. "It was an assignment, which did not go well. Although..." He paused a moment, remembering that he did enjoy some of the evening. "I could get used to attending balls featuring a free supper. The lobster patties were especially good," he added, deciding not to mention that they were the only food he'd had a chance to sample. "Tell me, what got Fitz' knickers in a bunch?"

His first mate shook his head. "You weren't on board 'afore ten. Said you missed curfew and were therefore 'unfit to command,' I believe were his words."

Furrowing a brow, Blake thought the sailing master might have had a point. He *had* missed curfew —ten o'clock on the nights before they were due to sail—by over three hours.

"Nothing will come of the challenge," Nelson continued. "Besides, none of the crew will vote for him." Having just learned the week before that Blake neither owned the *Molly* nor had been—or ever would be—a pirate, Nelson was still feeling a bit bamboozled.

How had he not known?

"They had better not," Blake groused. This particular crew was made up almost entirely of men of his choosing, and although some had worked on ships owned by pirates in their past—and most of them for the prior captain of the *Molly*—all knew that the *Molly* was more of a ship of opportunity than an usurper of other ships' bounties.

Unless those bounties were illegal. Then they were fair game.

Nelson gave a shrug. He had served on the *Molly* for several years under the prior captain, Jack Crawley, and had never suspected Jack was anything other than what he appeared to be.

A man of opportunity.

One whose opportunities resulted in generous pay and shared spoils for those under his command. Nelson had purchased a seaside cottage in Yorkshire with what he earned on just two long tours with the former captain. Someday, when he was done sailing, he would retire to the cottage. In the meantime, it provided a home for his widowed sister and two nephews.

As for the former captain, Crawley had worn the black costume of a pirate ship's captain with ease. Adorned with gold chains and sporting a gold-capped tooth, Crawley really did strike fear in the hearts of those whose ships they boarded. Smugglers and competing pirates knew to steer clear of the *Molly*, lest their cargo be seized.

Smugglers were arrested. Liquors were confiscated. Pirates were put out of business.

And then, a most unfortunate incident occurred.

While on a mission to locate a missing duke in

the Cyclades, Captain Jack Crawley met a young woman and fell in love.

Not unfortunate for Nelson, of course. Crawley's retirement allowed for advancement. Nelson was now the first mate.

Nor was it unfortunate for the duke, who was found and returned—unharmed—to British shores. But for the crew of the *Molly*, it meant saying their farewells to a man whom they had grown to like and respect over the years he had commanded the ship.

Blake Russell, the first mate at the time, had taken command at the insistence of Matthew Fitzsimmons, Viscount Chamberlain, the head of the Foreign Office. Meanwhile, the crew had been led to believe Blake had purchased the *Molly* from Jack.

No one suspected the ship was really the property of the British Navy.

Blake had also taken command because he was the only other crewman who worked for the Foreign Service. Nelson also knew that Jack Crawley now went by a completely different moniker when on English soil.

Alexander Bradley.

The man's current command was of a large wooden desk in the War Office in Horseguards.

The mere thought of being stuck behind a desk

and spending entire days indoors had Nelson shuddering.

Meanwhile, Blake considered what the *Molly* was scheduled to do on this day. By the time the sun reached its zenith, the ship would be in the Channel in search of a French smuggler of brandy wine who had apparently been ferrying the liquor and hiding the casks in a cave just north of Suffolk's coast.

A knock had Blake and Nelson turning their attention to the door of the captain's quarters. "Come!" Blake called out.

The ship's youngest crewman, Flinn, appeared just beyond the half-opened door. "Message for you, Capt'n," he said, breathless as he held out a sealed missive. "A man in blue and green livery delivered it."

"Livery?" Blake repeated, just before he remembered they were still in dock at Wapping but scheduled to depart within the hour—the tide was nearly at its lowest.

He took the missive and immediately noted the seal stamped in the red wax on the back.

Chamberlain.

Blake cursed and broke the seal, wondering how his letter detailing last night's failure could have already been delivered—and replied to by the viscount—so quickly. He had sent it with a caddy to the Foreign Office only the hour before.

Unfolding the missive, a sense of foreboding accompanied the alarm he felt.

Russell,

There's been a kidnapping. Daughter of Sir Peter Wycliff, a baronet of some considerable wealth. No terms have been received, but a servant who followed the kidnapper reports she was taken aboard the Tuscan under cover of darkness. Report says the ship set sail at dawn this morning. Probable destinations include Calais and Le Havre. Ship is also known to sail the Mediterranean.

Assignment: Pursue, retrieve, and return Miss Wycliff to British shores at earliest. Cargo identity is need-to-know only. Pay for delivery to Parkenhurst House will be in British pounds.

Chamberlain.

Cursing, Blake remembered what had happened the night before. Baronet Wycliff's coach had left Weatherstone's mansion in a hurry, he thought with Miss Wycliff inside. Now he realized it was probably carrying the lady's maid.

So who had made off with Miss Wycliff?

With his Little Bo Peep?

A memory of Lord Dorchester's coach speeding away came to him in a flash.

Indignation had him inhaling slowly. Had Dorchester sailed off with the lust of his life? The baron had aimed a number of quelling glances in his direction the night before. Perhaps his attentions toward the baronet's daughter had delayed the baron's plan.

He gave a shake of his head.

He had been watching Dorchester to ensure he didn't get away with something of value from Lord Weatherstone's mansion.

Blake blinked.

Miss Barbara Wycliff was something of value. Her father was rich. A kidnapper could demand...

"Dammit!" Blake shouted to no one in particular. Those in his quarters all gave a start at hearing his curse, however, and straightened to attention.

Dorchester—or whoever it was who had made off with his Little Bo Peep—wouldn't get far, he vowed to himself.

He turned his attention on his first mate. "Sails up. Get us out of here and to the Channel. Now."

"Aye, Capt'n." Knowing better than to question a command, Nelson was up and out of the captain's quarters as fast as his short stature would allow.

Blake turned his attention to Flinn. "Find the *Tuscan*. They left port at dawn with illegal cargo, and we're going to get it back."

"Aye, sir." Flinn paused a moment. "Under which ensign, Capt'n?"

Blake inhaled and considered the options. They had flags for any number of countries as well as the skull and crossbones. "British, for now," he replied. He dared not take a chance at being shot at by a British naval vessel until they were well into the Channel.

Flinn hurried off in the direction of the main mast. The smallest of the *Molly's* crew, he was also quick-witted and eagle-eyed. As a barrelman, his job required he spend most of his time up atop the main mast in the crow's nest with a spyglass.

He paused at the base of the mast to assist the hungover sailing master, Fitz, with hoisting the main sail, and then clambered up the main mast. Once in the crow's nest, he began his survey of nearby ships, intent on locating someone who might know about the *Tuscan*.

Spotting a porter on one of the docks, he called out a greeting. When the young man acknowledged him, Flinn yelled, "Did you see the *Tuscan* this morning?"

The porter shook his head, but he pointed to another dockworker and repeated the query.

"Took off at dawn. Wasn't yet low tide, even. Headed north, followed by the usual departures."

Flinn called out his thanks and wondered why the *Tuscan's* captain would leave Wapping before low tide.

He tested the wind. The early morning departure of so many ships meant the *Tuscan* wouldn't have been able to move very quickly. That, and the lack of wind and the tides that morning would mean slow going for a sailing vessel.

Whistling to Fitz, Flinn called down what he had learned from the porter. Fitz acknowledged the news and headed to the captain's quarters.

*M*oving to the only table in his cabin, Blake unrolled a map of the Channel and traced the usual routes to Calais and Le Havre. If the *Tuscan* also sailed the Mediterranean, it was possible Calais would be but a brief stop before the ship headed to the Gates of Gibraltar. If the *Molly* didn't catch up to her before then, perhaps it could at the Gates.

Thank the gods the quartermaster had filled the hold with provisions the day before. They had enough to last at least a fortnight at sea. Enough to travel the two-thousand miles to the Cyclades if the winds favored the *Molly*.

Blake rather hoped they wouldn't have to go that far. He didn't want to lose another crew member to a Greek girl.

A slight shudder beneath his feet told him the

Molly was no longer moored at the dock. Shouts on deck made it apparent they had cleared the other ships. A few minutes later, and he knew they were headed east toward the Channel.

When Nelson returned to the captain's quarters, Blake glanced up from the map. "Ever heard of the *Tuscan?*"

Nelson furrowed a brow. "Bimmington's ship?"

Blake gave a start. Captain Bimmington wasn't known for smuggling, let alone kidnapping daughters of the wealthy.

"Fell into the hands of a frog privateer for a time, but it's back to sailing under a British flag, far as I know," Nelson murmured as he drew a hand over his short beard.

His brows furrowing, Blake allowed a sigh of frustration.

Had someone commandeered Bimmington's ship?

Or didn't he know he was carrying contraband cargo?

Perhaps the captain had fallen on hard times and had taken a bribe to look the other way. Or he had given his command to another while he spent time in the capital on shore leave.

Or someone had stolen his ship.

This last seemed highly unlikely, though.

Whatever the situation, Blake decided he couldn't

rely on the ship's captain to be of any help once they found the *Tuscan*.

A knock had the two turning to find Fitz in the doorway. "Beggin' the captain's pardon, but Flinn says the *Tuscan* left at dawn, headed toward the Channel, low wind."

Blake exchanged glances with Nelson and arched a brow. "Noted. Now do you care to explain why you're challenging me for command of this ship?"

Fitz' eyes widened. "Beggin' your pardon, Captain?"

Nelson did his best to suppress a grin. "Told ya."

"I don't want command of the *Molly*," Fitz said, his jaw slack.

"Then you might want to lay off the rum after one or two shots," Blake replied.

Fitz blinked. "Yes, Captain." He turned to go and then paused. "Is that cutlass new, Captain?"

Chuckling, Nelson pointed to the door. "Get the sails up, damn you."

His eyes widening, Fitz nodded and hurried out. When the door closed, Blake turned his attention to his first mate.

"Crowded docks that time of the mornin'," Blake murmured.

"Bimmington still has almost a four-hour head start on us," Nelson replied. "But we'll be faster by half or more once we're out on the Channel."

Another knock at the door had them turning their attention to find Fitz had returned. "Pardon the interruption, Captain, but..." He sighed and scratched his ear.

"What is it?"

"I found a stowaway, Captain."

Blake blinked. "Stowaway?" he repeated. For the entire time he had served on the *Molly*, there had never been a stowaway.

"She says she was sent by a Mr. Wycliff."

Imagining a distraught mother determined to find her daughter, Blake rolled his eyes. "How the hell did she get on board?" he muttered, not expecting an answer.

"By way of the ramp, Captain. She came aboard before Blakely saw to pulling it up on board. She has papers."

Papers?

"I'll see to this," Nelson said, making his way to the door.

Blake gave a shake of his head. A woman on board a ship would be nothing but trouble. Although his crew had enjoyed a few days of shore leave, the presence of a female didn't bode well. Of course, if she was an old crone, he wouldn't have anything to be concerned about.

Probably.

When the door opened again, he took one look and groaned.

CHAPTER 3
A MAID TELLS A TALE

Miss Althea Woodcock paused on the threshold of the captain's cabin and dipped a curtsy. "How do?" she said, her gaze darting between the two men who stared at her. "I brought an important paper for Captain Russell. I wondered if you could direct me to where I might find him?"

At learning they had a stowaway, Blake had hoped it might be an operative from the Foreign Office. Someone with more details about the kidnapping. But the young woman who stood before him definitely wasn't employed by the Foreign Office. In fact, her serviceable frock and drab redingote suggested she was a servant rather than a relative of Miss Barbara Wycliff.

He was about to tell her she had found him when her eyes widened.

"Blake?"

Blake blinked.

Nelson's eyes widened as he mouthed 'Blake' and gave his captain an appreciative glance.

Ignoring his first mate, Blake regarded the young woman in an attempt to remember how she had been dressed the night before. She had obviously been at the ball, for who else would know him by his given name? He hadn't used it in years.

Imagining the young woman with a mask covering her eyes, Blake realized she was Miss Wycliff's lady's maid. "I'm Captain Russell," he said, stepping forward to give a bow. "It is good to see you again, miss, although I wish it could be under better circumstances."

"Miss Woodcock," she replied, holding out a hand in anticipation of shaking the captain's. "So good to see you again, too." Her gaze took in his mode of dress and her eyes widened in shock. "You really are a pirate!"

Blake shook his head. "Hardly," he said as he reached for one of her gloved hands and lifted it to his lips. He brushed them over the cotton. "Miss Woodcock," he acknowledged. Out of the corner of his eye, he noticed Nelson staring at the young woman, almost as if *he* recognized her.

"Mr. Wycliff asked that I give this to you," she

said as she held out a folded letter. "It was delivered to Parkenhurst House whilst the baronet was at Chamberlain House. Sir Peter insisted it be brought to you as soon as possible."

Taking the proffered missive, Blake regarded the woman a moment. He was about to ask why the footman who had delivered Chamberlain's earlier note hadn't brought this one, too, but then he realized Mr. Wycliff wouldn't have known of it until his return home from meeting with Viscount Chamberlain. Since Wycliff has been at Chamberlain House—probably well before dawn—it meant he must have been introduced to Viscount Chamberlain in the past.

Perhaps they were friends, or attended the same men's club. No baronet—no matter how rich—would pay a call on the head of the Foreign Office in the middle of the night otherwise.

But why send a female courier? Surely a footman would have been a better choice to bring the letter.

As if Miss Woodcock could divine his inner thoughts, she said, "I am Miss Wycliff's lady's maid. I..." Here she paused and allowed a sigh that suggested sorrow. "I was the one who followed the kidnapper from Lord Weatherstone's mansion last night," she explained. "Thank heavens the Wycliff coach was nearby when that evil man took my mistress. And that our driver was able to keep up. But he couldn't overtake the kidnapper's coach, and before I quite knew what was happening, the rogue was carrying my mistress up the ramp to the *Tuscan*."

Blake's eyes widened. "You *saw* him?"

He once again remembered how Wycliff's coach had sped away from Weatherstone's mansion in pursuit of another coach. Oh, how he wished he had made it out of the mansion just a few minutes earlier than he did! Then he might have foiled the kidnapping before it could happen.

Althea nodded, but gave a slight roll of her eyes. "Except that it was a costume ball, so he was masked, as was my lady. He never removed his mask, even after he stole her away."

"I don't suppose he introduced himself?" Even before he finished asking the question, Blake knew what the answer would be. No man would be allowed to simply introduce himself to a young lady—he would have to request that someone else do the introductions.

Which wasn't exactly true in his case with Little Bo Peep, but then *she* had initiated their introduction.

"He did not, but..." Althea allowed a sigh. "I cannot help but think he seemed... *familiar*."

Although the comment had Blake about to ask why, he was more curious as to how the lady's maid ended up at a *ton* costume ball. Little Bo Peep, or rather, Miss Wycliff, had mentioned something about the lady's maid. Something about 'who would know?', but his attention had been so arrested by the young woman, he couldn't remember if she gave a reason. "Why exactly were you there?"

A blush colored Althea's face and she dipped her head. "My mistress... she wished for company, and she needed a chaperone. She asked that I join her. Since everyone there was to be wearing a mask, she said no one would be the wiser. But a man recognized her, because he approached her after a dance and offered her a glass of champagne."

"How do you know he recognized her?"

"He addressed her by name, sir. All proper like." She frowned. "I had a mind to follow that man up the ramp of the *Tuscan*, but the driver wouldn't hear of it. He took me back to Parkenhurst House right quick so I could tell Sir Peter."

"Good thing you didn't board that ship," Blake said, "or Sir Peter wouldn't have had any warning."

The lady's maid didn't seem placated, though, and she dipped her head in despair. "I fear my lady will be *ruined*," she whispered.

"Not if no one but us knows about this," Blake countered as he popped the wax seal on the letter. Unfolding it, he held it up to the light from the cabin's only window. Squinting, he struggled to read the messy, masculine script before he held it out to Nelson. "Can you make out these words?" he asked.

As if he'd been pulled from a trance, Nelson took the letter and studied the script for a moment. "It's the ransom note, and given its time of delivery, I would say our kidnapper arranged its arrival at precisely the right time to ensure the *Tuscan* would already be on its way into the Channel."

"To where?"

"Calais, according to this. Payment in the sum of twenty-thousand pounds is to be brought to the *Le Chariot Royal*, a coaching inn, I think it says, in *Rue Edmond Roche*," he murmured, struggling with the French words. "No later than seven o'clock this evening." Nelson allowed a low whistle as he turned his attention back on Blake. He stood up and rushed to the door. "I'll let Flinn know where to direct his spyglass," he said before he disappeared.

Althea watched him go before she turned her attention back on Blake. "You will get my mistress back?"

Blake nodded. "Oh, yes. With any luck and a good wind, we'll get her before the *Tuscan* puts into port at Calais," he assured her, feeling a bit of pride when he saw her reaction of relief.

The oddest sensation had his heart clenching just then. Until they reached the *Tuscan*, Miss Barbara

Wycliff was in danger. In danger of losing her virtue. Of losing her life.

The thought of beheading her kidnapper with his cutlass gave him a sense of purpose. How dare the cur take off with his Little Bo Peep?

Then Blake noticed how the lady's maid reacted to his claim. She was obviously impressed at what they intended to do, so he thought to temper her reaction just a bit. "I don't suppose Sir Peter gave you the twenty-thousand pounds for the ransom?" he half-asked. If the *Molly* hadn't been available, would the baronet have already boarded a fast ship with the intention of making it to Calais by the deadline?

Her eyes rounding in shock, Althea shook her head. "I should think not. Why, I cannot imagine he will be able to procure such a large sum on such short notice." Her eyes darted to one side. "Unless he happens to keep that much blunt in his study," she added.

Almost as if she knew he did.

Blake frowned, deciding to ignore the comment. Her words simply reinforced the need to intercept the *Tuscan* before it put into port at Calais. Since Chamberlain had dispatched them to find Miss Wycliff, he rather doubted the baronet had any intention of sailing to Calais today. "In the meantime..."

In the meantime? What was he supposed to do

with the lady's maid? Or rather, what was she to do for the entire day? At their current speed, they probably wouldn't make it to Calais until three or four in the afternoon.

"If I might be allowed, may I simply watch from the railing?" she asked. "I promise to stay out of the way of your men."

Furrowing a brow, Blake gave her query some thought. "The wind is especially strong," he warned.

"I don't mind. I'll just eat a bit of breakfast. Cook sent me off with some food," she replied as she indicated her overstuffed reticule. "Said it would help in case I experienced seasickness."

The mention of food had Blake's stomach growling, which reminded him that he hadn't yet made it down to the mess for breakfast. Last evening's lobster patties hadn't lasted much beyond the supper dance. "Very well. But should the wind get to be too much, you're welcome to return here," he offered. "Here. Let me escort you to the best vantage on the ship." He offered his arm, and, with a brilliant smile, Althea placed her arm on his, and they made their way to the railing at the bow.

CHAPTER 4

A RESOURCEFUL YOUNG WOMAN

eanwhile, on the Channel

Miss Barbara Wycliff knew something was wrong the moment her nose detected an unusual odor. Her bed linens had never smelled like this. Rank, with an undertone of salt and sweat. She wrinkled her nose in annoyance and moved her head, wondering why her neck hurt. Why her arms seemed to be pinned under her. Or were they behind her?

Which way was up?

I didn't have but one glass of champagne, she thought as she experimentally moved one finger and felt something coarse. Coarse and not the least bit pleasant surrounding her wrists.

Even her worst bracelet—the silver bracelet her older brother had bestowed on her for her sixteenth birthday—wasn't as bad as what she was wearing now. And that poor excuse for jewelry had been relegated to the back of her jewel box the day after she had opened the velvet pouch, sure it wasn't made by any of the silversmiths in Ludgate Hill.

How could her brother think she would like the hideous design of intertwined vines with leaves that protruded in every direction? Those very pointy leaves threatening to impale her delicate, pale skin at every turn of her wrist? Why, she couldn't even wear it with any of her ballgowns lest she stab herself in the middle of a cotillion or snag the fine silk of her ball-gown. Even her dance partner would be at risk of injury.

The floor seemed to drop from beneath her for a moment, only to lift back into place, and Barbara feared she might be sick.

One glass of champagne?

Could champagne really have her this uncomfortable?

The sound of a distant voice—definitely belonging to a member of the opposite sex—had her straining her ears. It didn't sound like one of the footmen of Parkenhurst House, nor the butler. Which had her opening one eye.

Her head lifted, and she hissed at the pain she felt in her neck. Had she fallen asleep in the coach on the way home from the ball? If so, this had to be the ugliest coach in which she had ever ridden.

What happened to the sky blue velvet that lined her father's town coach? To the comfortable squabs that provided a modicum of comfort whilst she was whisked from home to the London entertainments during the Season?

The floor seemed to move again, and Barbara opened both her eyes.

She inhaled sharply, immediately determining she wasn't in a town coach, nor a filthy hackney, nor even a conveyance at all. At least not one that was seeing to getting her home from the Weatherstone's costume ball.

The attempt to raise a hand to her face was met with resistance she just then realized wasn't due to her brother's hideous choice of jewelry, but rather bindings that held her wrists behind her back.

The urge to put forth an unladylike curse was too strong to ignore. *"Damnation,"* she whispered hoarsely. She turned her head to the left and right, relieved to at least see a window, although very little light came from it. She was sitting, but not in velvet squabs. She was on a chair, and not one built for comfort.

When she leaned forward to stand, she found she couldn't. At least, not easily. She bent forward and lifted, prevented from straightening completely due to the combination of her hands being bound behind her back and around the chair's back. Turning around, she allowed another curse when she confirmed she wasn't in a coach or even a hackney.

"*Damnation!*"

This time, the curse was more audible.

A door opened, and the stale air swirled around her as she turned to discover a man dressed in evening wear regarding her with an expression of amusement.

"Nothing about this is amusing, sir," she stated, one of her feet attempting to stomp on the rough wooden boards beneath her black satin slippers.

The move made no noise, nor did it cause any vibration in the floor, which only annoyed her more. Barbara let out a sound of frustration. Knowing she looked ridiculous, dressed as Little Bo Peep and all bent over and bound to a chair, she leaned back and bent her knees until the chair legs made contact with the floor, and then she sat down with a huff.

"I suppose not," the man agreed, straightening once he was through the small opening and completely inside the tiny room.

Barbara stared at the tall man, a combination of fear and annoyance keeping her from replying. At first, she had no idea who he was, which meant they hadn't been properly introduced. But his evening clothes suggested he hadn't made it to his home after his evening entertainments, either. Studying his clothes more closely, and then imagining him wearing a black mask, had her realizing she *had* seen him at the costume ball the night before.

"This should all be over by the end of the day," he said in a most reasonable manner.

"*This?*" she repeated, wincing when she realized she had spoken.

"It's a nasty business, I know. But it's necessary if I'm to gain enough to cover my expenses for the next year. I figure twenty-thousand pounds should be enough," he drawled as he pretended to study his fingernails. "Word has already been sent to your father."

Furrowing her brown brows, Barbara regarded the well-dressed man a moment as she considered his words. "We've not been introduced," she remarked.

His eyes darting to one side, as if he was giving her comment its due, he gave his head a shake. "We have not," he agreed, just as the floor beneath them shifted.

The motion had Barbara realizing she wasn't on solid ground, but rather on water.

She had been on a sailing ship once, back when her parents had taken her to the Kingdom of the Two Sicilies for a month. After a few days, she had adjusted to the constant up and down motion of the water. Welcomed it at night, when it lulled her to sleep. Tolerated it during the daylight hours between meals, when she thought she might toss up whatever she had last eaten.

Odd that she didn't experience any seasickness during the meals. Which had her realizing she was about to be sick.

"Is there something to eat?" she asked, ignoring the comment about her father. At least, at first. Was he referring to money for a ransom? Had she been kidnapped? From Lord Weatherstone's costume ball, no less?

"I can have a tray delivered," he offered.

She arched an eyebrow. "Now?" She glanced around, in search of a bucket. "I don't feel so well," she added, making sure she appeared as pale as possible.

It wasn't difficult.

She glanced down at her mode of dress and winced. She had thought her decision to dress as Little Bo Peep inspired, but this costume wasn't going to serve her well on this day. She had chosen the gown because it was perfect for her wide hips and trim waist. On a ship manned by, well, *men*—and no chaperone in sight—she might well be ruined.

Which had her wondering what might have

become of her lady's maid. Woodcock had been with her at the ball, appropriately dressed in the gown Barbara should have been wearing. Her ornate mask had prevented anyone from guessing she was a servant.

"What of the woman I was with at the ball? My... companion?" When Aunt Lilly had sent word her gout had flared up and wouldn't allow her to attend the masked ball, Barbara had thought to simply stay at home. But Woodcock had been quick with her suggestion that she be allowed to go in Aunt Lilly's stead. If anyone asked the maid to dance, she would feign an injured foot or only accept an offer for an English country dance she knew.

An arched brow preceded the kidnapper's response. "I'm quite sure I don't know who you mean." He frowned then, apparently noticing for the first time that Barbara really *was* on the verge of being sick.

He quickly disappeared through the doorway, and a different man, this one most definitely a sailor, given his swarthy complexion, unusual mode of mismatched dress, and missing teeth, entered carrying a bucket.

His odor alone had Barbara gagging.

"Mornin', miss," he said as he set the bucket next to her chair. "Cook's workin' on breakfast—cackle fruit and whatnot—but I can bring porridge right quick."

Barbara stared at the sailor, amazed she could understand his strange accent. "Yes. Please do," she replied. "And could you inform your captain that I've been kidnapped and bound to this chair with the most uncomfortable means of restraint? I really insist they be removed, especially since I'll need my hands to eat."

The sailor's eyes widened and then darted to one side. "Why, I think he knows, miss."

"Oh, good. Because Lord Dorchester is due to call on me at two-o'clock this afternoon, and I shouldn't want to miss my opportunity for a ride in the park with him. I get so few of them, you see," she said as she angled her head to one side.

Truth be told, she knew Lord Dorchester's reasoning for taking her to Hyde Park at two o'clock instead of the fashionable hour of five o'clock was probably because he didn't wish to be seen in her company.

Most of her suitors wanted to avoid being seen with her. To be seen with her in polite Society suggested a desperation found only in men who needed funds to cover debts—or just funds in general.

She wasn't a beauty by any stretch of the imagination. Although she had long, brown hair, it was a brown of indistinguishable characteristics. No golden streaks or red highlights. No natural curls or waves that made it easy for her lady's maid to dress. Just straight, mousy brown tresses.

Her broad face didn't help, either. Although she had wide-set eyes that might be considered exotic, the rest of her face was merely that. A face. Normal lips, unfortunately not of a rosebud shape. Cheeks that weren't enhanced by high cheekbones or a natural pinkish coloring. A nose that wasn't upturned nor hooked nor thin. A chin that might have been a bit on the pointy side, if not for the slightly squarishness at the very end that helped to soften the effect.

No, she was not a beauty.

But she was rich.

At least, her father was. Her dowry meant she had any number of gorgeous young bucks paying calls and filling her dance cards.

Just not openly courting her.

Thank the gods her father could afford the very best modiste and fashions to be had in London. She might not be the most attractive young lady at a *ton* ball, but at least she could be the best dressed, even if her gowns had to be specially made to accommodate her oversized bosom and wide hips.

If ever there was a body perfect for childbearing—

and a gown suitable to play the role of Little Bo Peep —she knew she possessed it.

What else could she offer a prospective husband?

Her seasickness forgotten, Barbara frowned at the sailor. "Well, if the captain knows, then why am I still here?" she asked, a hint of annoyance coloring her words.

The sailor blinked. "Can't say as I know, miss," he replied. Then, before she could ask anything else, he disappeared—or rather, escaped—through the door, and Barbara was once again left alone.

She reviewed his words in her head. *The captain knew.* And since he knew and hadn't come to her rescue, then perhaps he was in on the kidnapping!

Or maybe he had been kidnapped, too!

Barbara's stomach growled, reminding her it was morning. A quick glance in the direction of what she now knew was a porthole confirmed the sun had come up. As to how high, she had no idea.

She regarded the door, thinking the sailor hadn't secured it with any sort of locking mechanism. If she could just lean forward again and get to her feet, she might be able to waddle in that direction. Getting rid of the chair would help immensely, but how to get the hard back to slide out from between her back and her arms would be tricky.

She pushed her arms back as far as they would go

and then winced when she saw how her bosom pressed up above the neckline of her dress. Despite the danger of falling out of her gown, Barbara leaned forward and wiggled her arms.

She could feel the chair back slowly give way, and she took a few tiny steps forward until the front legs of the wooden chair caught on the floor and the back gave way from her arms.

Once she was free, she bent one leg so the chair wouldn't go clattering to the floor, her slippered foot catching the front of it and lowering it until the edge was just inches from the floor. She quickly stepped forward and winced when the chair-back caught the back of her skirts. At least the chair didn't make much noise when it finally landed on the wooden planks.

Once again surveying the room—the light from the porthole was definitely brighter now—Barbara sorted from the barrels and crates that were stacked on one side that she she was in some sort of storage room. Then, when she turned to see a cot and small wardrobe on the opposite wall, she gave a sound of protest.

Am I supposed to sleep on that? she wondered, her nose crinkling at the mussed linens. The thought that they had put her into someone's cabin almost had her feeling sick again.

She regarded the bucket and the chair. Thought of her hands behind her back.

Well, she could at least make her arms more comfortable. She bent her knees and squatted down as far as she could and then fell back on her bum, grimacing when she realized the wooden floor probably hadn't been cleaned since the boat was built. Then she leaned to one side and pulled one arm forward before rocking to the other side and doing the same with her other arm.

Cursing at how difficult it was to get her arms around her hips, she continued rocking side to side and pulling her arms forward until they were beneath her thighs. Once her knees were bent up to her chin —or at least her bosom—she was able to work her bound hands beneath her legs and feet and around the gown and petticoats. When her arms were finally in front of her, she let out the breath she'd been holding and cursed.

The binding was twine, which explained the coarseness, but at least the ends were slip-knotted. She grimaced as she used her teeth to pull on the ends, and then gave a sound of disgust when the knot was finally free and she had to push the offensive material away from her mouth with her tongue.

Wincing, Barbara rubbed her wrists. At least her

silk gloves, now ruined, had prevented the twine from directly touching her skin.

She scrambled to her feet and shook out her skirts. A quick look through the porthole showed water for almost as far as she could see, although there might have been a hint of the cliffs of southern England in the distance.

Or was that some other land mass?

Barbara blinked. Had they been on the water that long? She remembered the man's comment about this being over by this evening.

Over *where*, though? Where was he taking her? And how was her father supposed to find her?

Marching to the door, she opened it a crack and peeked out. Cooking scents—and not good ones—assaulted her nostrils, but no one seemed to be on the part of the deck she could see. Opening the door wider, she leaned out and decided the entire crew must have gone to the mess for breakfast.

Was this ship even large enough to include a mess?

She slipped out, inhaling the fresh air with appreciation. Glancing left and right and finding the deck clear, she closed the door as quietly as she could manage and then made her way to the starboard rail. A few steps more toward the bow, and she was able to hide behind what she had just then come to realize was the captain's quarters.

Had the man no self-respect? His quarters were filthy. Even before she could conclude what might have happened to her given the lack of a chaperone, Barbara took stock of her bearings.

South.

The ship was definitely sailing south, which meant it would either land in France, or turn east and make its way out to sea. Another option had it following the coast around to the Straits of Gibraltar.

The thought of open water had her stomach churning. She had made the trip to the Kingdom of the Two Sicilies with her parents when she was fourteen years of age. She loved Rome and Florence, Naples and Venice. But she had wished for death when the ship sailed on the Mediterranean.

This was not good.

Especially because, even though she was no longer tied to a chair in the captain's quarters, she had no place to go.

She thought briefly of commandeering a life raft, but details such as how to get into it, how to get it into the water, and then how to row it had her deciding she was better off finding a place to hide.

Or should she just return to the captain's cabin and await the delivery of breakfast?

CHAPTER 5
IN PURSUIT

*M*eanwhile

With a British ensign flying from the top mast, the *Molly* made its way out of the Thames and into the Channel. The ship was barely past the cliffs of Dover when white caps promised a rough crossing. The wind had picked up, and although that boded well for their speed of travel, it didn't make Flinn's job very easy.

The spyglass held to his eye, Flinn surveyed the line where the sky met the sea, struggling to concentrate on the southern horizon as the ship rocked and bucked. The sails on their third mast had been deployed once they had passed Botany Bay, and their speed had nearly achieved its maximum when Walmer Castle came into view.

The ships that had clogged the Thames earlier that morning had spread out on the water, their paths forming a sort of blooming flower. Some headed north, their cargo intended for Newcastle or Edinburgh. Some headed directly across the North Sea to Belgium or The Netherlands. Most fanned out to the south.

Knowing the *Tuscan* was a British merchant vessel —a brig with sixteen guns—Flinn ignored the ships that were clearly Portuguese, Spanish, or French in origin. Their distinctive profiles made them easy to detect, so he instead concentrated on English ships.

Able to spot a ship nearly twenty-five miles away from his perch in the crow's nest, Flinn aimed the spyglass in the direction of France and hoped their prey really was headed for one of the French ports.

Hearing his name shouted from below had Flinn giving a start. He lowered the spyglass and looked down to discover Captain Russell standing on the deck with his hands on his hips.

"Their destination is definitely Calais!" Blake called out.

Flinn grimaced before yelling, "Aye, Captain. No sign of the *Tuscan*." He glanced at the position of the sun—nearly directly above them—and added, "but we're still an hour from a likely sighting." He had been gauging their speed from familiar landmarks, impressed by just how fast the *Molly* could travel when speed was necessary. The wind favored them, but that meant it favored the *Tuscan*, as well. The two-masted ship couldn't begin to match their speed, though, especially if she was loaded with cargo.

Blake allowed a sigh that could almost be heard by Flinn. "If you see any ship that might be the *Tuscan*—"

"I'll give a shout, I promise, Captain," he yelled down.

Blake allowed a nod. He knew he could count on his crew. They had trained under Jack Crawley. Been paid well for their services. Continued their service under his command for nearly a year. And although this mission wouldn't see their hold filled with contraband liquor or valuables, they would be paid a reward by Sir Peter—in blunt that would allow his men to enjoy a quick shore leave and as many prostitutes as they could employ when they finally went off in pursuit of the French smuggler.

The thought of spending time in the company of a willing woman had Blake allowing another sigh. Although he had enjoyed the company of women in numerous ports of call—Rome, Barcelona, Algiers, Le Havre—he found he no longer looked forward to time spent with the prostitutes who saw to sailors.

He thought of Jack, or rather Alexander Bradley, the former captain of the *Molly*. Blake remembered how Alex had been dumbstruck by the sight of a young Greek woman on the docks at Mykonos. Dumbstruck and struck by Cupid's arrow, for Bradley had fallen in love with the woman. The two had been wed while at sea as the *Molly* made its way back to London.

At the time, Blake had been dumbstruck by his captain's behavior. How could a man decide he had met the love of his life after spending only a few hours in her company?

What had him believing she was the *one?*

Blake gave a shake of his head. The night before, he had experienced lust at first sight, but that wasn't the same as love at first sight. He didn't believe in love at first sight. At least, not as it applied to a woman he might decide was the one. If he ever took a wife—and he wasn't convinced he ever would—it would be after courting her for several weeks. And after he had decided to retire from captaining the *Molly*.

Captains of ships were rarely married men.

But the thought of Miss Barbara Wycliff had him reconsidering for just a moment. Dressed as Little Bo Peep, her charms on prominent display and her red lips smiling easily, Barbara seemed like the perfect woman to come home to after a few days away at sea.

The kiss they had shared, although brief, was filled with as much passion as was possible. If he had the chance to repeat it, he vowed he would do so. Then he might allow his lips to trail down her neck and past her collar bones to the generous breasts below.

The thought of cupping one in his large hand, of how it might feel to caress the velvet soft skin as she pressed it into his hold, of how he might flick his thumb over the engorged nipple, had the oddest sound escaping his throat.

He dared a glance at Nelson, wondering when his first mate might be ready to take on the piloting of the *Molly*. At learning the ship was really under the command of the Foreign Office, Nelson had seemed to take the news in stride. Almost as if he had already known the *Molly* wasn't really a pirate ship. Which meant he would make the best choice for captain once Blake decided to retire from service to King and Country.

That is, if the man could get his eyes back in their sockets. Ever since their stowaway first appeared on the threshold of his quarters, the first mate had stared at her as if he were seeing a ghost.

And not a frightening one.

Did the two have history? Or had Cupid's arrow struck his first mate?

Blake wasn't sure he wanted to know, but until they had the *Tuscan* in their sights, he had nothing better to do than to discover what he could about the young woman.

And Little Bo Peep, as well.

CHAPTER 6
HIDING IN PLAIN SIGHT

*M*eanwhile, back on the Tuscan Barbara inhaled deeply as she concentrated on the horizon. As long as she stared at something that didn't move, she could keep her seasickness in check. With the wind whipping the sails, she didn't hear the man who approached from the bow.

"Since you're up and about, I trust you're feeling better, my lady?"

Jerking her head to the right, she immediately regretted the move, for her stomach lurched. "I was," she hedged, noting the man seemed to have recently bathed and wore a white shirt with a waistcoat and cape coat over Nankeen breeches. A tricorn hat hid most of his graying hair. His slight beard was the only feature out of place for a man who appeared to be a gentleman. "I... I don't believe we've met."

"Cyrus Bimmington, miss. I'm the captain of the *Tuscan*." He held out his right hand. "You were asleep when you were brought on board, but given the early hour and your illness, it only stands to reason you would be."

Furrowing a brow and giving her head a shake, she asked, "Do you do this often?"

"Cross the Channel? A couple of times a week, usually," he replied. "Not always to Calais, though, but since your husband has offered—"

"Husband?" she repeated, her eyes rounding in disbelief. "If you're referring to the cur who left me tied to a chair in your quarters, let me assure you he is *not* my husband."

The captain stepped back, obviously surprised by the vehemence in her words. "Tied to a chair?" he repeated before his own eyes rounded. "Well, I don't wish to get in the middle of a lover's quarrel—"

"Lover's quarrel?" Barbara had to forcibly close her mouth and consider that she probably sounded like a parrot to the captain. At that thought, her gaze darted to the left and then to the right, wondering where his parrot might be.

Didn't sea captains keep parrots as pets? Or did only pirates do such a thing?

"Captain Bimmington, let me assure you in no uncertain terms that I am *not* on this ship because I wish to be."

The older man angled his head back and forth. "I understand. Unexpected travel, because he forgot to inform you of his plans. Sometimes my fellow men can be difficult to live with. Give him a chance to apologize—"

"Sir. I have been *kidnapped*," Barbara stated, her hands moving to her hips. The move had the captain reacting, but not in the way she expected. Her generous bosom had not only lifted considerably, but it was also thrust out so that his gaze settled on it with appreciation.

"Oh, my sweet. There you are."

Barbara's eyes narrowed, and she turned to find her kidnapper displaying a pleasant expression. "How *dare* you. I am not your *sweet*. And now that the captain knows that I've been kidnapped, I'm quite sure he'll turn this boat around and head back to London. Lord Dorchester is calling on me this afternoon, and I intend to be at home when he does."

The captain and the kidnapper regarded one another for a moment before they both burst out laughing. "I rather doubt a *lord* would be paying a call on a young woman who is clearly of a lower class than he," the kidnapper remarked. And then his eyes widened. "Unless he's calling for a different reason," he added, his hips thrusting forward in a suggestive manner.

He didn't see Barbara's hand before it impacted his cheek.

He did see stars afterwards, however.

"How *dare* you, you... *rogue!*"

The kidnapper was about to retaliate with a hit of his own, but Captain Bimmington stepped in between the two with his hands held up, palms out. "Now, now, you two," he said in his most soothing voice. "Perhaps, Mr. Smith, it would be best if the missus ate her breakfast now," he suggested.

"I am *not* his wife!" Barbara responded, her voice raised so that several deckhands paused in their duties and turned to stare at her.

"You will be considered thoroughly ruined, however," Mr. Smith hissed under his breath.

Barbara heard the comment and once again felt ill. She turned her attention on the captain, but realized he would be of no help. "Would you have the time?"

Bimmington pulled a pocket watch out of his waistcoat, gave it a quick glance, and said, "Half-past nine."

"What will it take for you to turn this boat around?"

Inhaling as he gave a glance in the direction of the well-dressed gentleman, he said, "Passage to Calais has already been paid, milady. For you both. The winds favor us in this direction, but they will not going back to London."

"How much?"

The captain furrowed a brow. "How much?"

"How much will it cost my father for you to turn this..." She glanced up and noted the two masts and six sails. "This ship around?" she asked.

Exchanging glances with the kidnapper, Bimmington shook his head. "As I said—"

"He told me my ransom is twenty-thousand pounds," she said as she lifted her head in the cur's direction.

"Now, my sweet, it's evident you're not feeling well at all..." Mr. Smith managed to duck just before her fist flew past his head.

Once again, Captain Bimmington stepped between them, his arms held out as if he could provide some sort of wall between them. "Perhaps it would be best if the two of you spent the rest of the trip at opposite ends of this ship," he warned, his manner far more serious than it had been. He gave a nod in the direction of a beefy deckhand, who immediately moved to join them.

"Captain?"

"Escort Mr. Smith to the poop deck."

"Aye, Captain."

"This is an outrage," the kidnapper argued, his anger directed at both Barbara and the captain. "I paid for passage—"

"Then you can remain in your cabin for the rest of the voyage," Bimmington warned, a bushy eyebrow arched up.

Mr. Smith directed a fierce look in Barbara's direction. "If you think this is over—" He didn't have a chance to complete his threat before the beefy deckhand grabbed him by his cravat and nearly lifted him from his feet. Any protest he tried to make was caught in his throat as he was practically dragged away.

Barbara let out a breath of relief. "Thank you, Captain," she said. "Now can we turn back for London?"

Bimmington shook his head. "If you weren't so ill, I would send you back to my cabin for the rest of the trip," he replied. "Instead, I order you to eat your porridge and remain near the bow."

Her eyes widening in disbelief, Barbara shook her head. "But, I've no hat. No parasol," she argued.

Rolling his eyes, the captain said, "I'll get you an umbrella. Will that do?"

About to argue further, Barbara realized the

captain was through with abiding his troublesome passengers. "It will have to," she replied on a sigh. Then, just because she thought to sow some more seeds of doubt in the captain, she added, "I am my father's favorite daughter. He's a baronet, you see." She angled her head, deciding he didn't need to know that she was her father's *only* daughter. "Sir Peter. He's a very rich baronet, which is why Mr. *Smith* kidnapped me from Lord Weatherstone's masked ball last night. Seems he requires a good deal of money to make his living—"

"Enough, Miss..." His eyebrow arched up when he realized she hadn't introduced herself.

"Wycliff. Barbara Wycliff," she replied.

Although he looked a bit uncertain for just a moment, Bimmington gave a shake of his head. "Never heard of a Peter Wycliff," he said.

And with that, he strode off in the direction of the wheelhouse. The short, stout deckhand that she had spoken to earlier in the captain's cabin stepped up carrying a tray on which rested a bowl of porridge. Porridge that had obviously congealed in the time she and Mr. Smith had been arguing with the captain.

"Breakfast, my lady," he said as he held out the tray.

Her stomach once again making its displeasure apparent, Barbara took the tray and thanked the man.

Moving closer to the bow, she held the tray over one arm as she picked up the spoon, rubbed it on a pink satin sleeve, and then tucked into the porridge.

Despite the fact that it was no longer hot, she thought it was the best tasting porridge she had ever eaten.

CHAPTER 7

A DOUBTFUL CAPTAIN

Once he was in the wheelhouse, Captain Cyrus Bimmington regarded his first mate with a worried expression. "Tell me, Anders. Ever heard of a baronet by the name of Peter Wycliff?"

Anders stepped aside so the captain could take the wheel. "Sir Peter?" he replied. "The owner of Wycliff Mercantile? Wycliff Drapers? Wycliff Textiles? And the new owner of the shopping arcade in Bond Street? That Peter Wycliff?"

Bimmington stared at his first mate for perhaps a moment too long, for the man continued with, "Did he buy this ship, too?"

Seeds of doubt now fully sown, Bimmington shook his head. "Not that I'm aware."

"I heard he was in negotiations to buy Wilson's fleet," Anders countered, with too much enthusiasm.

"What do you know of his daughter?"

His eyes darting to one side—Anders prided himself on knowing everything he could of important people in London—he furrowed a brow. "Barbara?" he countered, as if he was making a guess.

Bimmington rolled his eyes. "She cannot be," he murmured. "She's dressed no better than a barmaid."

Anders allowed his captain to ruminate for a moment before he asked, "Would you be referring to the young lady that our passenger brought on board before dawn?" he asked. "The one who is dressed like Little Bo Peep? Her mask must have cost a fortune, what with all that gold gilt on it."

Bimmington blinked. "Aye," he replied carefully, just then remembering that Mr. Smith had been wearing a black mask when he stepped aboard carrying the young woman in pink. "Said she'd had too much champagne." Before he even completed the word, he thought it odd that a woman dressed in the clothes of a shepherdess would have had champagne.

"More like drugged," Anders countered.

Bimmington furrowed a brow. "Drugged?" He gave a huff. "Why didn't you say anything?" Now he really was beginning to wonder if there was some truth to the young lady's claims.

"Well, at first I thought she was dead," Anders replied. "Didn't want to be in trouble with some murderer. But then I heard her snore, so I figured she would be right as rain once she slept it off." When he saw his captain's look of disgust, he asked, "Do you think she's lying about who she is?"

"I have no idea what to think at the moment," Bimmington replied, but his furrowed brows and thoughtful expression were at odds with his comment.

One thing he knew for certain. If his passenger really was the daughter of a wealthy baronet, and if she really wasn't married to the man whom he knew as Mr. Smith, then it was rather likely someone would be looking for her.

Which meant, someone would be looking for the *Tuscan*.

"Have our barrelman keep watch to the north. I want to know if anyone is following us," he ordered.

Anders nodded. "Aye, Captain," before he hurried off to the main mast.

THERE'S SOMETHING ABOUT
A MAID

eanwhile, back on the Molly When Blake was sure Miss Woodcock was out of earshot—she had taken to watching the *Molly's* progress from the railing near the bow—he joined his first mate at the wheel. "You care to explain what's going on between you and the lady's maid?"

So stunned was he by the strange query, Nelson nearly let go of the wheel. "I'm sure I don't know what you mean, Capt'n," he replied.

"You know her."

Nelson straightened as much as he could, although the captain still had a good six inches on him. "I might," he hedged. When Blake lifted an eyebrow, as if that could coax the man to say more, Nelson allowed a huff. "But I might not."

The captain dared a glance at the lady's maid. When he was sure her attention was still on the horizon, he said, "You couldn't take your eyes off her when she was in my cabin. Am I right in thinking the *Molly* might be losing another crewman to Cupid's curse?"

His mouth dropping open and his eyes rounding in shock, Nelson did let go of the wheel. Blake quickly grabbed one of the spokes in a fist before it could turn and held it in place as his first mate fumed.

"First of all, Captain," Nelson said with a huff. "The chubby little bastard knows better than to waste an arrow on me, and second of all, she ain't what I'd be looking for to warm my bed, if you catch my meaning."

Blake furrowed both brows. "Oh, no, Mr. Nelson. I've seen what you do in nearly every port we pull into. Don't be trying to convince me you're some... *molly*," he warned, whispering the last word.

The comment only seemed to rankle his first mate even more. "I like my women... *fruitful*, Capt'n," he stated.

His eyes darting to one side, Blake was almost afraid to ask. But he did anyway. "Fruitful? What the hell does that even mean?"

Nelson's cupped hands went to his chest. "Peaches

up top, melons on the bottom, and a bright red cherry—"

"I get it!" Blake said in a hoarse whisper. A quick look in the direction of Miss Woodcock showed she wasn't well endowed up top—or on the bottom. As for whether or not there was a bright, red cherry, he wasn't about to guess. "Still, I saw you staring at her. If not because you were imagining a tumble with her, then pray tell, why?"

Taking the wheel back into his beefy hands, Nelson lowered his voice and said, "I ain't saying she is who I think she is, but if she is who I think she is, then I have to say I am verra curious as to how she landed a position as a lady's maid. That's all I'm sayin'."

When he didn't elaborate, Blake began tapping his black leather boot on the wooden planks below.

Nelson allowed an audible sigh. "I cannot be positive—"

"But if you were—"

"Then she'd be one of the grifters from my old neighborhood in Cheapside."

The captain's eyes widened before he allowed his gaze to sweep the horizon, which included another quick look at the lady's maid. "How the hell does a grifter become a lady's maid?" he half-asked. Didn't a servant have to show a character to be considered for employment? Be dispatched from an agency, or be referred by someone of importance?

"Exactly what I was thinking, Capt'n. Which is why..." Nelson stopped and allowed a sigh. "I'm expecting she might be trouble." His eyes narrowed as he stared at Miss Woodcock, who was now leaning against the railing with her back to the water. His expression quickly turned friendly when her gaze caught his, and she dipped her head in acknowledgement.

"Now, what you did just there," Blake said in a quiet voice. "That's what has me thinking Cupid got a clean shot."

Nelson rolled his eyes, and he was about to respond when a shout came from above. Blake moved to stand beneath the crow's nest. "Report!" he called out.

Leaning half out of the barrel, Flinn pointed southeast. "Found her! Six sails," he yelled. "Twenty, maybe one-and-twenty miles."

Waving up to the barrelman, Nelson turned so he could take a look at Miss Woodcock before he settled his attention on the captain. He wasn't surprised to find her attention had returned to the water. She had one gloved hand raised to her forehead to shield her eyes from the sun. As for her ability to catch sight of the *Tuscan*, Miss Woodcock wouldn't be able to see it for some time. The *Molly* would have to travel another half-hour or so before those on the deck would be able to spot the *Tuscan*.

"At this rate, we may not catch her until she almost pulls into port," Blake said under his breath. Although the winds had favored them through the mid-morning hours, they had subsided once the sun passed the zenith. "The last time we made this trip, we did so in four hours," he murmured.

"And it was twenty hours the time before that," Nelson reminded him.

Crossing the Channel could be problematic.

Blake nearly jumped out of his skin when he realized Miss Woodcock was standing to his right.

"Twenty hours?" she repeated in alarm. "Will we be in time to rescue Miss Wycliff?" she asked, her expression laced with concern.

Blake and Nelson exchanged quick glances. "Well, that's the plan, but even if we don't get her back—"

"We'll get her back for you, Miss Woodcock," Nelson interrupted. "Seeing as how you would be out of a position if we didn't."

The lady's maid's eyes widened. "Are you thinking my mistress is about to meet some dreadful end?"

The two men exchanged glances, and both shrugged their shoulders. "Hard to say," Blake replied.

"The sea can be a cruel mistress," Nelson added.

"There is a deadline. If the baronet doesn't get the money to the kidnapper by five o'clock..." Nelson used a finger to make a slicing motion across the front of his neck.

Blake was about to argue the time of the deadline, but realized Nelson was playing Miss Woodcock.

Didn't the first mate remember that she had been the one to deliver the ransom note? That she had heard Nelson reading the instructions, including the time? Given her widened eyes and pale complexion, though, perhaps she hadn't heard, or had merely forgotten the details of the exchange.

Blake decided to play along with his first mate. "Hard to believe the kidnapper thought the baronet could make the trip later in the day with the ransom. And such a large one."

Miss Woodcock, looking ever so horrified, turned a furrowed brow on the captain. "Well, why couldn't he?" she asked, her query sounding entirely innocent.

"Ship has to leave London at low tide. There isn't a ship at Wapping that would attempt to leave any later in the day," he explained. "We were barely able to make it out when we did."

When Nelson was about to remind the captain that there were steam ships that could make the trip, Blake stepped on his foot.

Her eyes widening once again, as if she was truly frightened, Althea visibly swallowed. "Then how will the baronet send the ransom?" she asked. "If you don't stop the *Tuscan*, we'll have to have the ransom to get Miss Wycliff back," she whined.

The two seamen exchanged glances. "You mean, *you* don't have it?" they asked in unison. Blake pointed down to her valise. "Seems like it would have been expeditious for Sir Peter to have sent it with you."

Miss Woodcock actually looked down at the valise as if she were seeing it for the first time. "These are clothes for my mistress," she replied. "She was taken from the masked ball dressed as Little Bo Peep. Hardly an appropriate gown for a baronet's daughter to wear for her trip back to England," she explained.

"Hardly," Blake agreed, although he rather liked Miss Wycliff as Little Bo Peep, all innocence despite a body meant to be worshipped by a man such as him. His lips would sprinkle kisses up and down her entire body. His mouth would feast on the mounds of her breasts, his teeth and tongue teasing her nipples into tight buds. Then his tongue would see to a most sensual delight, the tip of it circling her engorged womanhood until she begged for him. His cock, hard as a rock and soft as velvet, would dive into her wet, welcoming cocoon. Surrounded by her warmth, his cock would thrust and pulse and thrust again, until the friction sent him—and her—to a blissful state of euphoria.

Oh, the pleasures they could enjoy should they ever end up in a bed together!

Giving his head a shake and curious as to where those last thoughts had come from, Blake cleared his throat. He wondered if they had misjudged the lady's maid. Perhaps she really was a dedicated servant, and not the mastermind of an attempt to bilk a wealthy baronet out of twenty-thousand pounds.

"Not sure how the kidnapper expects to spend his blunt in France if it's all in British pounds," Blake remarked. "Not like he can exchange it in France, given the poor relations between the two countries, and he won't be able to return to England. Be arrested as soon as he steps foot on shore."

"As well he should be," Miss Woodcock stated, her curt nod punctuating her words.

At a loss as to what else he could say to have the lady's maid admitting to her involvement in the kidnapping, Blake finally allowed a shrug. "I suppose we'll need to count on a rescue at sea," he murmured.

Nelson furrowed a brow, thinking that had been the plan all along. His foot still stinging from having been trounced on by the captain, he allowed a nod. "I'll have Fitz mount the jib sails," he said.

Blake smirked, rather glad he didn't have to be the one to suggest they add their last two sails to their arsenal. "One hour, Mr. Nelson. Then I expect to be boarding the *Tuscan*."

"Aye, Capt'n."

CHAPTER 9

A SHIP PURSUED

eanwhile, on board the Tuscan

His crow's nest listing left and right with the rough seas beneath the *Tuscan*, the barrelman, Taylor, had a hard time keeping tabs on their pursuer. Either a ship really was after them, or it just happened to match their course for Calais.

One thing was certain—with seven sails and two jibs full of wind, it would be running into their stern within an hour. Given the British ensign flying from the main mast, he didn't think it posed a threat, though.

"Is that what I think it is?" Anders called up from where he stood on deck.

"British vessel," the barrelman called down. "In a hurry, from the looks of her sails."

Grimacing, Anders dared a glance at the wheelhouse and another toward the bow. Their female passenger stood gripping the railing in one gloved hand while she held an umbrella aloft with the other. If she really was Miss Barbara Wycliff as she claimed, then perhaps it would behoove them to simply slow down. They were ahead of the schedule their one paying passenger had detailed the night before—*get me to Calais by five o'clock in the evening*—so if the ship in their wake wasn't after them, it would simply beat them into port.

If it was after them, then there would no doubt be a warning shot fired from a cannon. Or worse. A cannon shot aimed to do their hull some damage.

The very last place he wanted to have to arrange repairs was a French sea port. They would be charged double or triple and be stuck in Calais for a fortnight or longer.

"I'll let the captain know," Anders called up. He turned and was about to head to the wheelhouse when the barrelman gave a shout.

"A pennon is going up," the barrelman called down. He gave his head a shake. "Red and white, and here comes another."

Anders stiffened, wishing his eyesight was better so that he could make out the shapes on the pennons that were rising to the top of the other ship's main mast. He hated relying on the barrelman to know their meaning. "Can you make out which ones?"

The barrelman whistled before he leaned over the edge of the crow's nest. "They wish to communicate. Apparently, we're in danger."

"Damnation!" Anders dared another glance at the ship that followed them and then allowed his gaze to sweep the horizon. There was no sign of an impending storm or another ship. The shoreline of France could only be seen when the *Tuscan* crested a wave.

Had France declared war again? Were they sailing into a trap by making port at Calais?

Or was the danger due to something else entirely?

He hurried off to the wheelhouse to speak with the captain.

When told about the ship in pursuit, Bimmington rolled his eyes. "Well, at least they had the decency to warn us with a pennon instead of a cannonball," he murmured.

"You think they mean to shoot at us?" Anders asked, stunned. "It's a British ship. Looks like a naval vessel leftover from the war."

Bimmington sighed in frustration. "They outman us, and they outgun us," he said in a low voice. "And I'm not about to take a cannonball because some cit paid too much for passage to Calais."

"What's this now?"

The captain and Anders both turned to discover their passenger, Mr. Smith, regarding them with a look of alarm.

"I was just telling my first mate here that I'm not looking to take on a cannibal because some Brit paid his passage to get away," Bimmington replied, as if he were repeating what he had said to Anders.

Mr. Smith blinked. "A cannibal?" he repeated, his eyes wide. "Is there such a thing?"

"In the West Indies, yes," Bimmington replied. "I think it's best they stay there. Now," he said as he crossed his arms once he knew Anders had the wheel. "Why aren't you where you belong?"

The cit who paid too much for passage to Calais straightened and then pointed to the stern. "I came to tell you a ship is coming up awfully fast on your tail."

"I am well aware," the captain replied. "They're carrying a message for us. They seem to think we're in danger. Would you know anything about that?"

Mr. Smith's eyes narrowed. "Danger?" he repeated. "I've no idea what you're talking about." His gaze swept the horizon in the direction of their travel, although he couldn't see much beyond where Miss Barbara Wycliff stood. Her arms were outstretched, an umbrella held up to shade her face from the sun, and her body was arched forward, as if she was the ship's figurehead.

He had a fleeting thought that if she wasn't careful, her generous bosom would pop out of her pink gown for everyone in France to see.

"Are you thinking what I'm thinking?" Bimmington asked, his gaze having settled on the backside of their pink-clad passenger.

"That she might very well pop out of her gown?" Mr. Smith countered with a smirk.

The captain frowned and turned his steely gaze on the man. "That *she* might be the one in danger," he said, his words clipped. He turned to Anders. "Could you have a word with *Mrs. Smith?* Let her know she might be in danger of falling off the ship should she continue what she's doing?"

"Aye, Captain," Anders said as he gave control of the wheel back to Bimmington. He made his way to the bow and gave a slight bow when the young woman noticed him.

"Oh, how do?" she said as she stepped back from the railing.

Almost disappointed that her generous bosom had not escaped the confines of her ridiculous pink gown, Anders said, "The captain thinks you might be in danger, Mrs. Smith."

Her eyes turned to slits. "My name is not *Mrs.*

Smith. I am Barbara Wycliff, daughter of Sir Peter Wycliff. I have been kidnapped and am being held for a ransom of twenty-thousand pounds," she recited, as if she had said the words too many times that day.

"Be that as it may, he's worried you might fall overboard should you lean too far forward like you was doing."

Barbara allowed a heavy sigh and turned around. Her eyes widened when she saw the bow of another ship was nearly abreast of the stern of the *Tuscan*. "Does that happen often out here?" she asked in awe. The other ship was so close, she could make out the faces of the crewmen on board.

Shouts of "pirates" could be heard from the other end of the *Tuscan*, followed by running feet hitting the wooden planks.

"Not usually, Mrs... Miss Wycliff," Anders replied, his own eyes wide. The other ship was nearly alongside them now, and one of their sails had been dropped so their speed slowed to match that of the *Tuscan's*. "Hang on," he warned. "In case they get too close and collide with us."

Barbara did as she was told, but her attention was on the crew aboard the other ship. On the man who was dressed as a pirate. Wearing a cutlass and looking ever so rakish as his gaze settled on her. Looking exactly the same as the pirate with whom she had danced the night before.

"Blake!" she called out, waving with the hand that didn't hold the umbrella.

"Barbara!" he shouted back. "Fear not, for I've come to save you!"

Fearing for his life, Anders blinked and stepped away from the young woman. He blinked again and hurried off to find the captain.

Apparently Miss Wycliff would be able to fend for herself.

CHAPTER 10

A DEVIL IS SPOTTED

A half hour earlier

Nelson watched his captain as Blake moved to the bow of the *Molly*, noting how the captain's expression indicated he recognized the lone, black-clad figure that stood at the stern of the *Tuscan*.

"Now you look as if *you're* seeing a ghost," he accused.

"That's because I am," Blake said as he pulled a spyglass from his eye. He handed it over to his first mate. "The *gentleman* standing at the rail. Recognize him?"

Nelson frowned before he lifted the spyglass to his eye. "Looks like a... like a gentleman," he murmured. "Should I know him?"

Blake took the instrument back, holding it to his eye and cursing as he watched Lord Dorchester struggle to light a cheroot. "That's the kidnapper," Blake said in a voice filled with menace. "Son of a biscuit eater took my Little Bo Peep right out from under me."

Blinking, Nelson furrowed a brow. "While you were having a tumble with her? Blimey!"

It was Blake's turn to blink. "No. Of course not. While I was at the costume ball. Looking for her. And for him. He disappeared, and so did she, and now I know why," he hissed. If he'd had a pistol on him, he would have aimed it in the direction of the baron and shot him.

"He took your Little Bo Peep?"

Blake stiffened, his anger growing by the moment. She wasn't really *his* Little Bo Peep, but he did want her. More than he realized when he had first learned he was to retrieve her. "Aye," he breathed.

Nelson gave the *Tuscan* passenger one more glance through the spyglass before handing it back to his captain. "Then it's time we go get her. Shall I fire a warning shot?"

"And risk injuring her?" Blake countered. "Absolutely not. Pull up alongside, and we'll forcibly board the *Tuscan*."

Amused more than alarmed by his captain's orders, Nelson said, "Aye, Capt'n. Should I hoist the skull and crossbones, too?"

Blake gave his first mate a quelling glance. "Not yet. But let them know we have a message. And tell them they're in danger," he ordered. They weren't really, but if the crew of the *Tuscan* didn't abide his instructions, he just might fire a warning shot. From a pistol he had stowed in his cabin.

Nelson hurried off to the main mast. He called up to Flinn, "Hoist the danger pennon and then put up the message pennon." He had half a mind to order the red flag be hoisted after that—*no quarter would be shown*—but decided that one might be too much.

Flinn made a motion signaling he understood. A few minutes later, the red and white flag indicating the other ship was sailing into danger crawled up the rope a few feet. Then it paused as Flinn attached the pennon conveying they had a message. The two flags climbed to near the top of the mast as he pulled the rope and then secured it.

"Can you make out anyone else on board?" Nelson called up.

A spyglass held to his eye, Flinn let out a shout. "I see something pink near the bow. Looks like..." He lowered the spyglass and gave his head a shake.

"Little Bo Beep?" Nelson offered.

Flinn leaned out of the crow's nest and flashed a huge grin. "I was going to say a tart dressed in pink, but, yeah, she could be Little Bo Peep. Although..."

He paused and waggled his eyebrows. "Her bosom's not so little, if you catch my meaning, but neither is her bum. And I don't see no sheep."

Nelson held back his curse. Didn't the barrelman know that Little Bo Peep had lost her sheep? The nursery rhyme his sister told to his nephews implied they were long gone before the story even started.

Instead of explaining the story just then, Nelson said, "The gent at the stern?"

"Yeah?" Flinn acknowledged.

"He's the kidnapper."

"He's on the move," Flinn warned, his gaze back on the *Tuscan* by way of his spyglass.

"Crikey," Nelson muttered, realizing just then the kidnapper might conclude the *Molly* was after him. He raced to the wheel to inform Blake.

CHAPTER 11

AN ARRESTING PROPOSITION

*B*lake Russell gauged the amount of space he would need to clear the Tuscan's hull and ordered the jib and top sail to come down. Noting how the captain of the *Tuscan* was following a near-straight course directed to the now-visible port at Calais, he felt confident the two ships wouldn't collide.

His crew's excitement was palpable. Once he had explained they were to rescue the young woman in pink—*she is not a tart, but rather the daughter of a rich baronet*, he had been quick to inform them—they rushed about on deck carrying out his orders.

The opportunity to earn their share of the blunt offered by Sir Peter might have been the primary reason for their enthusiasm, but Blake thought perhaps they were itching for action. Itching for an opportunity to wield their swords and play pirates for just a few minutes.

He'd had to remind his men that Lord Dorchester would need to be taken alive. The baron was a peer, and therefore untouchable when it came to his crime. Should the aristocrats in the House of Lords decide to try him, Blake hoped they might see to a suitable punishment. Stripping him of his title and tossing him into Newgate would be Blake's choice, but he didn't think the lords would see it the same way.

"Now should I have Flinn hoist the skull and crossbones?" Nelson asked when he joined Blake at the wheel. His question was laced with a bit too much enthusiasm.

"The Jolly Roger? I don't know that we have to do that," Blake replied. "We risk taking a ball from one of their guns."

"Bimmington won't shoot. He's already hoisted a white flag."

"What?" Blake quickly raised his gaze to take in the sight of a white pennon waving from the *Tuscan's* top mast. "Well, I'll be damned," he murmured. "I guess this means we won't have to scuttle the *Tuscan*." Not that he had been considering it, but if Captain Bimmington proved difficult or had fired on them, he would have given the order to return fire.

He then noticed an older gentleman waving from the starboard rail. Dressed in a navy topcoat festooned with brass buttons, his head topped with a black tricorn, Captain Bimmington was aiming a glare in his direction.

"Take the wheel," Blake ordered, his attention entirely on the other captain, "and raise the Jolly Roger. I want Dorchester to see it." The words were said with spite, and a grin touched Blake's lips.

Nelson did as he was told, a gleam in his eye. "Aye, Capt'n."

Blake made his way to the leeward rail. "Sorry about this, Captain," he called out. "But you're carrying contraband cargo and a kidnapper, and I've been hired to see to their retrieval and return to London."

Bimmington jerked at hearing the other captain's words. "My cargo is entirely legitimate—"

"All except for Little Bo Peep," Blake called back. "Give up Lord Dorchester, and give up the shepherdess, and no one gets hurt."

Giving his head a shake, Bimmington shouted, "On whose authority?"

Blake was tempted to yell back, "Mine," but instead said, "Lord Chamberlain, Foreign Office. You're transporting a kidnapper."

Dipping his head at learning the young lady had

been telling the truth, Bimmington was almost glad the other ship had intercepted his. Getting rid of Mr. Smith would be a relief. "Since I've already received pay for his passage, you can have him," Bimmington replied, his need to yell lessened now that ropes had been tossed from the *Molly* to the *Tuscan* to ensure the two ships stayed abreast of one another. "But you'll have to come get him. I rather doubt Mr. Smith will go willingly."

"You'll not fire on my crew?"

Bimmington shook his head. "We'll be glad to be rid of him."

Feeling a profound sense of relief, Blake called out the order to bring forth the planks that would connect the two ships. He hurried to the bow, relieved to see Barbara. She was apparently safe, holding an umbrella aloft and looking ever so pink in her Bo Peep costume. Although a bit wind-blown, she looked radiant when her gaze settled on him and recognition had her calling out his given name.

Never in his life had he felt such relief. Such joy. Such desire for a woman. No, she wasn't a diamond of the first water. Her features weren't those of an English beauty. Her eyes were a bit too far apart and rather large. Her chin nearly ended in a point but was saved by a bit of squarishness. Her brown hair, having long since lost its pins, was whipping about due to the wind and would no doubt resemble a rat's nest when she was safe aboard his ship. But her smile was infectious, and the sight of her pink-clad body had his reacting in a manner entirely inappropriate for the occasion.

"Barbara! Fear not, for I've come to save you," he called out.

What the hell? Had he really said such a thing? And out loud?

What the hell had gotten into him?

Miss Woodcock appeared at his side, the valise gripped in one hand and her smile wide. "My lady! I brought you a change of clothes," she yelled. And then her smile faltered. "I don't know that I'll be able to do anything with your hair, however."

Blake gave the lady's maid a quelling glance before he turned his attention back on Barbara. "I'm coming for you," he shouted, and made to head for the planks that now connected the two ships.

"Not unless you have twenty-thousand pounds!"

In the span of a blink of an eye, Lord Dorchester had moved up behind Barbara and had grasped her around the waist with one arm. He now held a pistol to her face, the barrel denting the rounded flesh of her cheek.

Alarm and fear had Blake frozen where he stood. "You unhand her this instant, you cur!"

"Not until I get the ransom and safe passage to Calais," Dorchester called back. In a voice that only Barbara could hear, he added, "Isn't this so much more exciting than our two o' clock ride in Hyde Park would have been?"

Barbara stiffened in his hold. "Lord Dorchester?" she whispered in awe, attempting to turn so she might see him more clearly. The gun barrel pushed harder though, and she was forced to look at Blake.

Which she didn't mind in the least. His concern for her seemed genuine.

He was dressed exactly as she remembered him from the night before, which meant he really was a pirate. Either that, or he had rushed off to his ship to save her the moment he learned she was in danger. Standing as he was, with one hand on the hilt of a cutlass and the other on his hip, he looked dangerous. Devilishly handsome, despite his large nose. And quite annoyed, given how the muscles at the top of his broad shoulders bunched.

"Oh, Blake," she whispered, wishing he could hear her words. "My hero." In a louder voice she said, "Don't give him a farthing."

"Now see here, you..."

The baron didn't have a chance to finish his curse when a brandy wine barrel came down hard on his head.

Holding it between his two hands was Fitz.

The *Molly's* sailing master stood over the crumpled body of the kidnapper for a moment in an effort to determine if he had really knocked him out before he raised his head and then gave Miss Wycliff a slight bow. "Miss Peep," he said with an impish grin. "'Tis verra good to meet you. My mum used to read me your rhyme next to me bed at night", he said in all seriousness. "Didn't realize you were real. So sorry about your sheep."

Barbara blinked. And blinked again. "Oh, well, thank you," she replied, adding a curtsy, just before she was suddenly engulfed in Blake's arms.

"Are you well? Did he hurt you?" the captain asked, not giving up his hold on the young woman.

"I am fine, now that you are here," Barbara murmured, rather liking how one of his hands was sliding down her backside. When he cupped her bottom and pulled her closer, she let out a gasp and her eyes widened. "Have you really come for me?" she asked in a whisper.

"I have, my lady," Blake whispered.

"However did you know where I was?"

Blake reluctantly pulled away but left his forehead pressed against hers. "I'll explain later, but first we must get you aboard the *Molly*. Take you back to London," he murmured. He raised his head and motioned toward Lord Dorchester. "Good work, Fitz. Tie his hands behind his back, and get him onto the *Molly*," he ordered.

"There's twine in the captain's cabin," Barbara suggested, and Fitz paused to nod at her before he hurried off.

Barbara returned her attention to Blake, her tremulous smile suggesting she might cry at any moment. "You came for me," she whispered.

Blake took a deep breath and let it out as he nodded. "I did. I was so worried. Did he... did he force himself on you?"

She shook her head. "No."

"I would shoot him if he did."

"You would do that for me?"

Nodding, Blake once again dropped his forehead to hers. "Are you sure he didn't hurt you?"

Barbara was almost disappointed when she had to say, "Yes, I am sure."

"Did he frighten you?"

Angling her head to one side, Barbara thought of the moment the pistol was shoved into her cheek. "Yes."

"Then I'll shoot him for that," Blake vowed.

A delightful grin spread over Barbara's face. "I believed you really were a pirate when I saw you a moment ago."

Blake aimed his attention on the boards that connected the two ships. "You may again when I tell you we have to walk the plank."

"What?" Despite the disbelief in her voice, Barbara allowed Blake to lead her to where the set of planks spanned the divide between the two decks. A wave of seasickness had her clutching her middle. "I cannot walk the plank," she managed to say.

Without a word of warning, Blake lifted his Bo Peep into his arms and strode across the chasm between the two ships, grinning when he saw how she had squeezed her eyes shut and wrapped her arms around his neck.

Once he was on the *Molly*, his crew broke out in cheers, and Barbara opened her eyes.

"That wasn't so bad now, was it?" he asked as he set her back on her feet.

She struggled to stand upright, and when Russell noticed, he simply scooped her back into his arms. He surveyed his crew, most agog at seeing him carrying a woman. "Take Dorchester to the brig. Get us back to London. We've a reward to collect for having captured him," he called out.

The crew erupted in another round of cheers before they scattered to do his bidding. The reward promised in Lord Chamberlain's letter was really for returning Miss Wycliff to her father, but his crew didn't need to know that.

And neither did Barbara.

CHAPTER 12
A MAID IS MISSING

With Barbara still in his arms, Blake headed towards his quarters.

"Where are you taking me?" she asked, her hands once again wrapping around his neck.

"To my... to the captain's quarters," he managed to say. "I've a comfortable chair for you, or there's a bed should you wish to lie down."

"Your bed?" she asked, sounding almost hopeful.

Blake swallowed. "Yes. Should our trip back to London take all night, then I will see to it you and your lady's maid—"

"Where is Woodcock?" Barbara asked, glancing back to where Althea had been standing with the valise. "I should like to get out of this costume and into warmer clothes."

"She's around here somewhere." Blake frowned,

wondering where the lady's maid was. "She has your valise—" He spun around, his gaze searching the area where he had last stood next to Althea, but that part of the deck was now abandoned.

He noted how Fitz and Blakely were seeing to Lord Dorchester, the two managing to haul the baron's prone body across the planks. Once they were on board the *Molly*, the wooden planks were pulled back onto the ship, and the ropes tying the two vessels together were loosened.

Captain Bimmington stood with his hands on his hips, watching closely as the *Molly* drifted away from the *Tuscan*, as if he was worried the two ships might yet collide. He gave a wave when it was apparent they were on separate courses. "May the wind be at your back," he called out.

Blake acknowledged the words with, "And at yours," before he carried Barbara into his cabin.

He set her on the edge of his bed. "I'll have your maid join you when I find her," he said as he straightened. In the dim light, he allowed his gaze to pause for a moment. Despite her mussed gown, the faded red lip color, and evidence she'd been exposed to wind and sun this day, her wide eyes were bright as she regarded him.

She still took his breath away.

Finding the temptation too great, Blake leaned down and kissed her.

Much like the kiss he had bestowed on her at the ball, Barbara wasn't expecting it, but she returned it without hesitation.

Blake finally pulled away, his heart hammering despite the excitement of the past half-hour having passed. "I know I should apologize—"

"Don't you dare," she warned with a shake of her head.

"Oh, well then." Blake took her face between his hands and kissed her again, this time for a moment longer. "I won't," he whispered before he gave a slight bow. "Please, make yourself comfortable. I've something I need to see to, but I will return soon." He took his leave of his quarters.

Barbara let out the breath she'd been holding, sad for the loss of his attentions but heartened that he had simply picked up where they had left off the night before at the ball.

Had that really just been the night before? So much had happened in such a short amount of time!

Rising to her feet, she took a few steps to test her balance. The motion of the water beneath the larger ship was less noticeable than on the *Tuscan*, and she walked with confidence to the door of the cabin to look out.

Deckhands were scrambling about, a few climbing ropes or pulling on them in an effort to get the *Molly* turned around for its trip back to London. That's when she noticed the pennon of the skull and crossbones flying above, the wind whipping the black and white flag so hard, she could hear the flapping sound.

"Pirates," she whispered. A combination of disbelief and fear gripped her just then. In all the excitement, she hadn't even noticed that Blake's ship really was a pirate ship.

A hand went to her middle again as she struggled with seasickness. Food. She really needed food. Determined to find some, she made her way down the only stairs she could find.

"*I*s she in here?" Blake asked when he stepped into the wheelhouse. Nelson was at the wheel, struggling to get the ship headed north.

"She who?" the first mate responded.

"Woodcock."

Nelson paused in his task and stared at the captain. "She was on deck a moment ago," he said as he pretended to look for the lady's maid. "She's not in here." He was about to say more, but the captain disappeared.

Blake rushed about the deck. Not finding Miss Woodcock along any of the railings, he stood beneath the main mast and called up to Flinn. "Where's the lady's maid?"

The barrelman leaned out of the crow's nest, his gaze sweeping the ship below. He then turned his attention on the *Tuscan*, and his arm shot out. "Over there," he called out. "On the *Tuscan*."

Blake turned around and then made his way to the stern, his attention on the lady's maid who now stood at the rail of the other ship. On the deck next to her feet was the valise. "What did you do?" he called out in confusion, realizing she had to have walked the plank to get onto the *Tuscan* when the two ships were still joined. Was she mad?

Or had she run a rig?

"I decided I wish to live in France," Althea shouted back, her shoulders shrugging in a manner suggesting she didn't have a care in the world. "Thank you for the ride." Her huge grin suggested she had made her decision long before she had boarded the *Molly*.

A niggling, annoying feeling had Blake cursing just then. He had really hoped she wasn't what Nelson had suspected, but it seemed his first mate was right. "With twenty thousand pounds, I suppose?" he yelled back.

The lady's maid dipped a curtsy and smiled again, but she said not a word. The distance between the two ships would have prevented her response from being heard.

"Dammit," Blake ground out. "Dammit all to hell."

Althea Woodcock had been in it with Lord Dorchester all along. She had probably been dispatched with the ransom by her employer, so that if a ship hadn't been able to intercept the *Tuscan* before it reached Calais, the ransom could still be paid.

Well, what would Sir Peter do when he discovered she had made off with his money? Money that was probably supposed to be the reward money for returning Barbara Wycliff to London?

Blake was pondering this and more when he returned to the wheelhouse to tell his first mate what he had discovered.

"Gone, isn't she?" Nelson asked when Blake joined him again.

Blake allowed a grimace, thinking his first mate seemed awfully pleased with himself. "On the *Tuscan*. With the valise, of course," he said on a long sigh. "Dammit, how is it she even made it over there without being seen?" he asked. "With twenty-thousand pounds, no less?"

Nelson allowed a grunt. "Oh, not with twenty-thousand pounds," he countered, a barely hidden smirk finally growing to display his slightly yellowed teeth.

Blake blinked. And blinked again. "What are you saying?"

His first mate gave a shrug. "That valise she's got with her isn't the same valise she came aboard with."

His brows furrowing in confusion, Blake gave a shake of his head. "It's not?" A flare of hope had him raising an eyebrow.

"Nope." Nelson reached down and then lifted a valise from the floor next to his feet. "This is the one she brought on board. Has clothes in it, just like she said, but there's more underneath. Lots more."

A grin slowly forming to replace his expression of distress, Blake said, "When you say lots more, are you referring to twenty-thousand pounds?"

One shoulder lifted as Nelson turned the wheel. "Can't say how much exactly, seein' as how I can't count that high," he replied. He set the valise back down at this feet.

"You dog."

Nelson held up a finger and waved it back and forth. "Now, now," he started to say before Blake had him in a bear hug.

"You were right to trust your instincts," the

captain said when he released the startled first mate. "You're going to make an excellent captain for this ship."

Furrowing a brow, Nelson eyed Blake for a moment. "Are you sayin' you're giving up the *Molly?*" he asked in disbelief.

Blake let out a breath, his thoughts on Barbara. For a few moments back in his cabin, he had imagined an entire life with her. Now that reality was making itself apparent again, perhaps his imaginings were folly.

Sir Peter probably wanted his daughter to marry an aristocrat. Or at the very least, a well-to-do cit. What would the baronet's reaction be when a mere ship's captain asked for permission to court his daughter?

"I had a thought perhaps it was time," Blake started to say. "But..." He allowed the sentence to trail off and shook his head. He glanced down at the valise. "If it's all right with you, I'll take that to my cabin. Miss Wycliff would really like to change into a proper gown."

"All right by me," Nelson replied, using the toe of his boot to push the bag in Blake's direction. "Just don't be getting any ideas."

The captain nodded. "If I remember right from that letter Woodcock brought on board, this very well may be our reward money," he said with a grin. "Split fifteen ways means we all get over..." He paused to do the math in his head. "Thirteen-hundred pounds."

"Don't be counting any chickens, Capt'n," Nelson warned.

Blake sobered. "Good point." He picked up the valise, but before he could turn and make his way back to his cabin, he paused and regarded Nelson with suspicion. "If this is the valise that Miss Woodcock was carrying when she came aboard, then what's in the valise that she took onto the *Tuscan?*"

Nelson's eyes lifted and then darted to the left and right. "A couple of old shirts," he murmured.

Frowning, Blake leaned against the doorframe. "And?" he prompted. He knew the other valise would have had to have more in it to make it as heavy as this one that Woodcock had brought on board. Otherwise, the lady's maid would have known the bag had been switched out with another.

"Oh, some potato peelings from tonight's dinner. Couple o' fish. Some old bread."

Blake rolled his eyes, almost hoping the lady's maid might discover the change in luggage and remain on the *Tuscan* for its trip back to London. If she made it to Calais and disembarked, she wouldn't have the means to pay for anything. "She was in on it with Dorchester, wasn't she?" he half-asked. Woodcock had probably helped arrange everything, including her last-minute substitution as a chaperone at the masked ball the night before.

Nelson allowed a shrug. "Probably."

How could I have been so blind? Blake wondered, remembering how Lord Dorchester and the lady's maid had been paired up for a dance the night before.

"Are you going to claim Miss Wycliff for yerself now?" Nelson asked.

Furrowing a brow, Blake was about to deny his first mate's query. But he knew there was one way he could ensure he ended up with the young woman.

It was not a very honorable way. He would risk the reward Lord Chamberlain implied would be paid upon his daughter's return. But the temptation was so great, he merely nodded in Nelson's direction and took his leave of the wheelhouse.

CHAPTER 13

A MAIDEN AND A CAPTAIN

In the captain's quarters

Surprised that it was Blake who came back into the cabin instead of Woodcock, Barbara stood up, a half-eaten slice of bread clutched in one hand and an apple core in the other. "Does that bag contain a change of clothes, I hope?"

Blake set the valise on the bed. "I think so," he replied as he leaned over and bussed her on the cheek. "There's more in here than clothes, though."

Barbara was quick to set aside the bread and apple before she opened the valise. Reaching in, she began pulling out coral fabric by the handfuls followed by yards of white muslin. "Well, at least she's brought my favorite gown. I'm quite over wearing pink." She looked up and then turned her attention to the closed door. "What have you done with my lady's maid?" she asked as she shook out the crepe de Naples gown and petticoats. "I'll need help with dressing."

Blake dipped his head. "Miss Woodcock... she boarded the *Tuscan* shortly after I brought you aboard. Seems she prefers France over England."

Her head jerking up, Barbara regarded Blake for a moment before she sat down on the bed. Hard. "Oh," she murmured, disappointment evident in her voice. Her eyes widening a moment later, she dropped her head into her hands. "Oh, no. Please tell me she wasn't part of this."

Blake immediately joined her on the bed, pulling her into his arms. "I'm so sorry, but I cannot. Did you have any idea she and Lord Dorchester were planning such a nefarious scheme?" he asked in a quiet voice.

The way her body shuddered, Blake knew Barbara was weeping. He felt her head shake against the small of his shoulder, and a quiet sob sounded.

"Nnn... no," she managed to get out. "How could she? How could she do such a thing?"

"How long has she been your lady's maid?"

There was a pause before Barbara sniffled and lifted her head from his shoulder. "A month, is all," she managed between sobs. "She came with the very best character, though. She was an upstairs maid in a mansion. A baron's mansion."

At the same moment Blake sorted the identity of

the baron, Barbara did as well. She shook her head and inhaled sharply. "The cur!"

"Indeed. They probably planned this long before she came into your employ," Blake reasoned. "Waiting until you were in need of a lady's maid just so she could be the first to apply."

Barbara rolled her eyes. "Althea Woodcock applied even before then. And she was the only one to do so," she put in, her attention on something far away. "No one else applied, at least as far as I know."

Furrowing a brow, Blake asked, "You say she applied before you were in need of a lady's maid?"

Nodding, Barbara regarded him a moment. "She had to have known my father was going to pension my former lady's maid. Cruthers was quite old, you see."

His brows still furrowed, Blake wondered at the timing of the kidnapping. Both the baron and the lady's maid had to have been in exactly the right places the night before in order to pull it off. Ordering the Wycliff coach to follow Dorchester's town coach had been brilliant—the driver would have been convinced of Woodcock's devotion to her mistress when she urged him to follow the Dorchester coach, especially when she attempted to board the *Tuscan*.

"Dorchester expected to get to Calais and then be

joined by Woodcock," Blake reasoned. "He must have known your father would either arrange a rescue or send the ransom." Peeking into the valise, he could see the mound of bank notes filling the bottom half. Never in his life had he seen so much blunt. "And that your father would trust Miss Woodcock with the ransom."

Barbara leaned over and stared into the bag. "Twenty-thousand pounds?" she whispered in disbelief. "I rather doubt he would trust her with this much money," she breathed.

Shrugging, Blake said, "I haven't counted it, of course, but I'll be sure to deliver it directly into your father's hands when I return you to Parkenhurst House."

A sense of melancholy settled over Barbara just then. She turned her back to him. "Since it seems I am without a lady's maid, could you undo the fastenings for me? I simply must get out of this gown," she said on a sigh.

Blake stared at the young lady's pink-clad back, noting how a row of laces held the edges together. Despite her request, he still paused before he undid the tie. Using a hooked finger, he carefully loosened the laces down to the base of her spine. Beneath her gown was an old-fashioned corset from the century prior. "I should probably... turn around whilst you undress," he murmured. He didn't, though, instead hoping she might ask him to continue undressing her.

Barbara gave him a glance over her shoulder. "So... you're not really a pirate?" she asked in a voice filled with disappointment.

Blake gave a start. Before he could answer, though, she added, "I saw the flag. The skull and crossbones. Doesn't that mean this is a pirate ship?"

Rolling his eyes, Blake gave a shake of his head. "That was... merely theatrics," he explained. "A way to strike fear in the crew of the *Tuscan*, since we didn't know if Captain Bimmington was aware of your circumstance or not."

Barbara huffed as she stood up and wiggled out of the wrinkled silk gown and a series of several ruffled petticoats. "He is quite a thick man," she groused.

The courtesy of standing whenever a woman did so ingrained into him, Blake stood up and did his best to keep his attention above her chest. When the words permeated his brain, he scowled. "Captain Bimmington?"

She nodded. "I explained in no uncertain terms that I was *not* married to Mr. Smith... Lord Dorchester, I mean," she corrected, "and yet, the captain seemed determined to believe that I was."

Her hands went to her hips, and it was everything

Blake could do not to reach out and pull her against the front of his body. The corset barely contained her generous bosom, and she wore a most scandalous pair of white silk drawers featuring several rows of ruffles around her knees. The white silk stockings that encased her calves had his gaze dropping to her ankles.

Well-turned ankles.

Blake swallowed. Hard. And then realized what she had said. Alarm had him pulling her into his arms. "Did Dorchester ruin you? Because if he did, I'll go down to the brig and beat him to a bloody—"

"He did not."

The words were so quiet, Blake dipped his head so that he could see more of her face. "Barbara?" he whispered, not even aware he used her Christian name.

"It would seem I'm not exactly worth ruining," she said on a long sigh. "In fact, I am beginning to believe my dowry may not be enough to convince any man to ruin me, let alone marry me," she said in a quiet voice.

"That's not true," he argued. "I would gladly ruin you."

Barbara blinked.

Blake inhaled sharply. "That is to say, I would be... I would be honored to... to ruin you."

"You would?" Her response was filled with surprise.

Pleasant surprise.

He boggled. "Well, I would be more honored if I could take you to wife, but..."

Barbara's eyes widened and then suspicion filled them. "Because of my dowry?"

Blake furrowed his brows and shook his head. "No."

Giving him a withering stare, Barbara countered with, "Then why?"

Blake sighed. "Because I'm rather... smitten with you."

She jerked in his arms. "You are?" Her words were filled with awe.

"I am." He took a breath and forged on. "But I am a commoner—"

"As am I."

"—and I rather doubt your father is going to give me permission to court you..."

"Court me?"

He nodded. "Well, of course. It would only be fair for you to learn more about me..."

Blake's words were stopped when Barbara's lips collided with his. His startlement lasted only a moment before he returned her kiss, reveling in her unbridled enthusiasm and the way she pressed the front of her body against his. His arms wrapped around her shoulders, and a moment later, he felt her fingers spear his dark hair.

When he finally pulled away—only enough to take a deep breath—he left his forehead pressed against hers. "You are in severe danger, my lady," he whispered.

"Really?" Barbara replied, with perhaps too much enthusiasm.

Blake straightened and regarded her with a smirk. "Why do I get the impression you *want* me to take your virtue?"

Dipping her head so his nose ended up in what was left of her messy bun, Barbara mewled, "Perhaps because I do. Ever since I met you last night—which now seems like weeks ago—I have wondered if you might be the one."

"The one?" he repeated.

She lifted her head and regarded him with an impish grin. "The one who might look beyond my rather rotund..."

"You are not rotund," Blake interrupted.

"Breasts," she continued, "and wide hips—"

"Your hips are perfect," he said, his hands moving to pull her lower body against his to reinforce his claim.

"And see me for who I really am."

He blinked. And blinked again. "Just so you're aware, I am in awe of your breasts." Leaning down, he kissed the tops of both in turn, knowing full well his silken hair tickled her shoulders. "And your hips." He squeezed her hips between his large hands. "And everything in between, and above..." He paused to kiss her forehead. "And below." He knelt and kissed each thigh just above the ruffles of her drawers, and then dropped his lips to the tops of her feet where he kissed them both.

Angling his head up, he saw how she stared down at him, an expression of awe etched on her face.

Blake knew he would never forget that look. And he knew exactly how he could ensure it stayed there. "If your father gives me permission, I shall ask for your hand," he whispered.

Barbara stared at him for a moment before finally blinking several times. "Oh, he will," she murmured. "I will see to it that he does." She placed her hands beneath his armpits and helped him to stand. "Do what you must to ruin me," she begged.

Blake made a sound not unlike a growl. "I cannot. Not yet," he added, noting the flash of anger that crossed her face. "But... I can... I can give you a... a *prelude* to what you might expect in our marriage bed," he stammered, almost immediately regretting the offer.

How the hell was he going to restrain himself? The mere suggestion that she wanted him to ruin her had his cock responding as if it were an emergency. Why, if they required another mast from which to fly a pennon, his cock would do in a pinch.

"A prelude?" she repeated.

Nodding, Blake reached behind her and tugged on the ties that held up her drawers. The white silk fabric dropped to the wooden planks below at the same moment she let out an "Oh!" She let out another when one of his hands smoothed over her mons and then dipped between her thighs.

She gasped, and her eyes darkened with understanding. "I really don't think I can stay stand..."

Barbara let out a cry of surprise as Blake lifted her up and then placed her onto the bed. He followed her down, his hand immediately returning to the moist curls hiding her womanhood.

"You're wearing far too many clothes," she complained.

Blake paused in his ministrations. "True," he acknowledged. He lifted himself from the bed just long enough to doff his waistcoat and shirt. At seeing Barbara's widened eyes, he glanced down his front. "Too much hair?" he asked, suddenly worried she might be offended.

Barbara shook her head. "I've just never seen a bare-chested man before," she replied.

She had, of course, but the memory of her as a young girl seeing her rather hirsute father in his dressing gown had her thinking that all men were as hairy as the bears she had seen in the menagerie at the Tower of London.

"I've a mind to remove your corset just because I don't believe you," he warned.

Her eyes widening in delight, Barbara said, "Oh, would you?"

Blake sighed. "You're going to make this easy, aren't you?"

She blinked, and then her eyes darted to one side. "Should I make it hard?" she countered, lifting herself to one elbow.

Grinning, he leaned over and kissed her. "I think I just fell in love with you," he whispered.

Barbara swallowed, stunned to hear his words. "Oh?" she breathed, well aware of where one of his hands had managed to move, his finger expertly inciting a series of rather pleasant tingles beneath her skin and then throughout her abdomen. For a moment, she wasn't sure she could breathe.

Wasn't sure she wanted to breathe.

Ever again.

Blake brushed his lips over her bare shoulder.

"What I mean to say is, I have been thinking about you every moment for the past—"

"Oh!" The word was quite loud, and Blake felt a profound sense of satisfaction as he repeated the ministration that had elicited the response. When she made the same sound, he knew he had her.

He worked his way down the front of her body, his lips pausing here and there to place light kisses wherever he could find bare skin. Although he had been given a clear invitation to ruin her, Blake had no intention of taking her virtue. His cock obviously hadn't gotten the message, given how it seemed to have a mind of its own. And perhaps a Jolly Roger attached to the end of it. The damned appendage wanted nothing more than to stake a claim inside her. Plunder and pillage and leave its treasure for a future visit.

Shaking the odd thoughts from his head—both of them—Blake settled his body between her spread legs.

Her invitation was apparent, and he wasn't about to send his regrets.

Replacing his fingers with his tongue, he proceeded to tease her womanhood with the tip of it. Delighting in her soft gasps and mewls of pleasure, he worked his tongue into the tight, wet space his cock was desperate to invade.

Fighting every thought of taking her virtue, Blake concentrated on bringing her to the edge of ecstasy. Concentrated on her thighs and how they pinned his head between them. Concentrated on how her body bucked beneath his hold.

And then, when he was sure she could take no more, he laved his tongue across her swollen womanhood.

Once.

Twice.

There was no third time. Barbara seemed to break apart beneath him, her once-rigid legs falling to the sides so her thighs were exposed to him. He took the opportunity to suckle each one for a moment, grinning when her mewling changed to an occasional whispered 'yes.'

When he was sure she'd had enough, Blake made his way back up her body, dropping kisses on her wrists and on the insides of her elbows. When he heard her giggle, he buried his head just above her breasts and allowed a long sigh.

Her fingers speared his hair, and he growled as her nails scraped his scalp and sent skitters of delight down the back of his neck. "You minx," he accused in a whisper.

Her hands stilled. "Is that... good? Or... bad?" she asked in a whisper.

Reluctantly, Blake lifted his head from her chest. "Good for me. Bad for your virtue, surely."

She grinned and returned her fingers to his hair. "Will you take my virtue?"

Nodding, because now there was no way he would allow anyone else to do so, Blake said, "I will, but not on this night. Not until I know for certain you are mine."

The words seemed to appease her, although he knew disappointment had settled over her. "Are you aware that once we are betrothed, I am at liberty to bed you?"

Barbara lifted her head, her disappointment replaced with hope. "You are?"

"I cannot believe I am saying this, but yes," he acknowledged. "Perhaps we can marry by special license, so you don't have to wait so long."

"You won't have to wait so long, either," she countered, a hand moving to cup the rigid member behind the placket of his breeches.

Blake jerked and groaned in response, his eyes closed lest he give in to his baser instincts. "True. So true."

They lay in companionable silence for a time, sleep nearly claiming them both.

"You'll sleep here tonight, of course," he

murmured. "I don't expect we'll make it back to London until early morning."

"And then what will happen?"

Blake frowned and tightened his hold on her. "I'll escort you to Parkenhurst House, of course. Explain to your father what happened, and give him the money."

"Is that all?"

He sighed. "I'll ask his permission to court you."

"And then?"

Sighing, Blake lifted his head from her chest and allowed a brilliant smile. "Then I shall file a report with my superior—I'll have to detail the events of this day—"

"All of them?" she asked in alarm.

"Well, all but those of the past hour or so," he replied. "Do not worry. I will keep you a secret, at least with my men."

She seemed to think on his words a moment. "Do you own this vessel?"

He shook his head. "I do not. I merely... captain it when we're sent on..." He sighed again.

Her brows furrowing, Barbara regarded him for a moment. "You're not really a pirate. But if you're not, then who sent you to find me?"

"Can you keep a secret?"

Barbara's eyes widened in delight. "Oh, I can, yes."

Blake nodded. "Well," he whispered as he offered her his right hand. "Blake Russell, Foreign Office."

She awkwardly shook his hand as understanding filled her eyes. "You were *sent* to find me?" Her head fell back on the pillow, as if she was offended.

"Trust me when I say I would have come after you even if I wasn't duty-bound to do so," he replied, hoping she wasn't disappointed. Perhaps she had been thinking he had been tracking her ever since she had disappeared from the ball the night before.

"So, if you're not a pirate—"

"I am the captain of a ship that pursues pirates and privateers, smugglers and such."

"Go on," she urged.

"I report to Lord Chamberlain, and the *Molly* is the property of the British Navy. Our mission is to capture smugglers, mostly, but occasionally I have to take on some rather unusual assignments, like this one."

"Hmm." She was quiet for a time. "And if we do marry, what will you do for a living?"

Blake thought of the discussion he'd had with Nelson earlier that morning.

Had it really only been that morning? The day seemed to have gone on for weeks.

"I think it might be time for me to consider a different living," he murmured. "Something a bit more land-based. Or more regular."

He couldn't believe what he was saying. He remembered feeling sorry for Alex Bradley, in that the former ship's captain was now piloting a desk in Horseguards.

"Won't you miss captaining a ship?" Barbara asked in a faint whisper. The cabin had grown dark with the sun having set, and without a candle lamp, the room was blanketed in dark grays.

"Possibly. But if I know I have you to come home to every day, I shall not mind so much."

Silence stretched for a time, and Blake thought perhaps Barbara had finally fallen asleep. About to lift himself from the bed to dress and return to the wheelhouse, he was prevented from doing so when she tightened her hold on him.

"My father is considering the purchase of some ships," she whispered. "Merchant ships, much like the *Tuscan*."

Blake blinked. "He is?" After listening to Nelson list all the properties Sir Peter already owned, Blake supposed he shouldn't be surprised the baronet wanted to increase his holdings.

"He'll need captains, of course," she hinted.

"But, I don't think I could bear to be away from you for weeks at a time," he reasoned.

Barbara shifted beneath him. "Perhaps I could... come along."

"You would do that?" Blake sat up and stared down at her. In the dark, he could barely make out her milky white skin against the dark blanket on the bed.

"I would. I tend to get seasick, but I haven't noticed it so much since I've been aboard this ship," she said, a hint of surprise in her voice.

"Probably because I've been keeping your mind off of it," he teased. He lowered his lips to hers. If only they could simply sail away. Enjoy one another's company by day and spend their nights making love under the stars. "I've a mind to stay with you all night."

He heard her slight hum and grinned when she said, "Then do so. I will not mind a bit."

Kissing her one last time, Blake sighed and dropped his head to her shoulder. When he was sure she was asleep, he slid off of her body, covered her with a blanket, and took his leave of the cabin.

Perhaps a discussion with his first mate would talk some sense into him.

CHAPTER 14

DISCUSSING A FIRST MATE'S POSSIBLE MATE

*M*eanwhile Turned around and headed back toward English shores, the *Molly* barely made any headway given the strong head winds.

"This may be one of those twenty-hour crossings," Nelson groused from where he stood at the wheel.

Fitz allowed a shrug. Given the events of the day, he didn't want to see it come to an end this soon. The sailing master had watched in wonder as their captain had rescued the pink-gowned maiden from the kidnapper. Marveled at how members of the crew had joined together to escort the baron to the brig and see to it he was made as uncomfortable as possible. Enjoyed the camaraderie as his mates ate supper and drank ale.

He still couldn't believe he had challenged the

captain for command of the ship just two nights ago. How could he have been such a fool, even in a drunk state? "I don't think the captain minds if it takes a week to get back to London," he said in response.

Nelson gave him a quelling glance. "You know what this means?"

His brows furrowed, Fitz gave a shake of his head. "Captain's not going to give up command of the *Molly*. Even if he gets the girl. And given her father's one of the richest men in all of London, I doubt he'll be allowed to marry her," the sailing master reasoned.

Rather impressed by Fitz's response, Nelson glanced in the direction of the captain's quarters. Blake and the young woman had been in there—without an escort—ever since they had left the *Tuscan*.

The details of the kidnapping would be kept a secret, or at least as much of one as was possible given the crew of the *Tuscan* knew as much as anyone on the *Molly*, so Miss Wycliff's reputation wouldn't suffer.

If she spent much longer in Blake's cabin, she would be thoroughly ruined, though. Perhaps that was his captain's plan. Ruin Little Bo Peep so her father would have to agree to allow him to marry her.

The scoundrel.

Nelson gave a shake of his head. They had just

had a discussion about not getting married. How could so much change in only two days?

With Lord Dorchester locked in the brig below deck and Miss Woodcock in Calais, her only possessions a couple of his shirts, two dead fish, and a sack of potato peelings, Nelson knew there was nothing else to be done until they reached Wapping.

He thought of the missive from Lord Chamberlain and finally allowed a grin. "We'll have a decent payday from this run," he said, hoping the promise of blunt would be enough to satisfy his captain if he didn't get the girl.

"Truth be told, I'd almost do this for nothin'," Fitz replied, his attention aimed north. "Long as I have a place to sleep and food to eat."

Nelson blinked. "Well, ain't you a model sailor?" he teased. But he understood the young man's sentiment.

And then a thought of Miss Woodcock had his own cock threatening to rise.

He gave his head a shake. What the hell? She wasn't what he found the least bit appealing, so why did thoughts of her come unbidden? Especially when she had turned out to be a thief?

"You're thinking of that lady's maid again, aren't you?" Fitz teased.

Nelson immediately leaned forward in an effort to

hide the bulge that was growing in his nether region. "Am not."

Fitz didn't even try to hide his smirk. "She was smitten with you," he countered. "Said she used to know you back when you were a pickpocket, and the two of you used to work the crowds at the pleasure gardens."

His eyes widening in alarm, Nelson lifted his finger to his lips. "Don't be spreading those lies," he warned.

Fitz merely rolled his eyes. "She said you would say that. She was impressed by how far you've come. Said she had to struggle as a maid for a long time 'afore she was able to get hired on as a lady's maid. Only because her mistress isn't some diamond of the first water. So she was really scar't when Miss Wycliff was taken. Thought she'd be out of a position. So I guess I'm as surprised as anyone she would choose France over coming back with us to England."

Nelson pretended like he was only half-listening to what the sailing master had to say. "How much time did you have to spend in her company to learn all that twaddle?"

"No more than half-hour. Right nice woman, she was. Might have to keep her in mind in case I decide to give up the sea." He watched the first mate, expecting a reaction.

He wasn't disappointed.

"Now see here, you fool. The woman was a thief," Nelson argued.

"Yeah. Stole yer heart, she did," Fitz countered.

Reeling at the sailing master's words, Nelson was about to put voice to a protest. Instead, he glanced in the direction of France and frowned. "What's this?"

A set of sails, barely visible on the darkening horizon, appeared to rise from the sea.

"I'll get Flinn," Fitz offered, knowing the barrelman was eating supper below deck.

Nelson was about to tell him not to bother. He was fairly sure he knew the identity of the ship that followed in their wake. But Flinn was already scrambling down the steep companionway.

In the growing gloom of twilight, his attention went to the door of the captain's quarters. He hadn't expected to see Blake Russell until morning, but the captain emerged and made his way toward him.

"I see the wind is not in our favor," Blake commented.

"Would've thought you'd be happy for it," Nelson countered.

Sure he heard a bitter note in his first mate's voice, Blake said, "I haven't ruined her if that's what you're thinking. We've been... talking."

"Talking?" The word was said with a good deal of disbelief.

"About our future, and what I might do should Sir Peter allow me to court his daughter."

Nelson blinked. "Court? You?" His eyes darted left and then right before he gave a shake of his head. "Where is Captain Russell? I demand to know. What have you done with him?"

Despite the first mate's serious demeanor, Blake allowed a chuckle. "He's been replaced, it seems."

"Say it isn't so," Nelson demanded.

Blake allowed a shrug. "Dammit, man, I think I'm in love," he whispered hoarsely.

"Lust, you mean. I saw how your eyes drift to her rather generous charms," Nelson argued. Blake acted as if he couldn't hear his first mate.

"Me! I never would have guessed it could happen, but I'm living proof that Cupid doesn't spare anyone."

Nelson nearly gave up his hold on the wheel. "The chubby urchin better keep his arrows in his quiver when it comes to me," he warned.

Blake allowed a throaty laugh. "He's coming for you," he warned with a grin.

"Oh, so you think he's on that ship?" Nelson asked as he pointed south.

Blake followed the direction of Nelson's finger and furrowed a brow. "I'll be damned," he murmured.

"How the hell are they making such good time?" For now that the ship that was following them had cleared the horizon, it was clear it was the *Tuscan*.

"They must have decided they didn't want a stowaway," Nelson commented.

"Which means they may want to give her back," Blake teased, although the thought of ever seeing the double-crossing lady's maid wasn't one he relished.

Giving him a quelling glance, Nelson added, "And they're traveling light. No cargo, so I guess it stands to reason they can make good time."

"Or Miss Woodcock discovered what was in the valise and begged them to bring her back to London," Blake countered. "You have good instincts, Nelson. You were right about her."

The first mate dipped his head. "Was I?"

Blake regarded the shorter man with a look that emphasized his confusion. "What are you implying?"

Nelson rolled his eyes and reluctantly shared a snippet of a conversation he'd had with the lady's maid earlier that day.

"You believe her?" the captain asked as his gaze once again went to the *Tuscan*. This new information certainly provided another reason for Miss Woodcock to have fled the ship.

Shaking his head in frustration, Nelson said, "I don't know that I do or I don't."

Nodding his understanding, Blake offered to take the wheel. "Why don't you get some sleep? At least until they make their intentions known?"

Nelson gave a glance in the direction of the captain's quarters. "Don't you have someone to entertain?"

Sighing, Blake was about to agree to Nelson's unspoken offer. Instead, he said, "I am still captain of this ship, and I'm quite sure my guest is sound asleep."

Nelson gave a nod and said, "Then good night, Capt'n." He disappeared down the companionway leaving Blake to ruminate on what would come next.

CHAPTER 15

REFLECTIONS ON A PIRATE'S PLEASURE

eanwhile, in the captain's cabin

Barbara knew the moment Blake had left the bed and his cabin, for it was the same moment she experienced a sense of loss. The heavy warmth of the captain's body along one side of her own lifted away and was replaced with a blanket that smelled of wool and Blake's cologne.

Had he thought her fast to allow him to pleasure her as he did? She should have pushed him away. Put up a fight, or at least a word of discouragement. Insisted she be left alone until their return to London.

But had she done so, her body would never forgive her.

How had the man managed to endear himself to her so completely after only a few minutes of conversation and a couple of dances?

With his clever repartee, of course. And the way he looked at her. Not like the way every other man saw her. Blake Russell didn't seem put off by her fleshy breasts or wide hips or her lack of beauty. In fact, he had seemed enthralled by her, even when she had shed her Bo Peep gown and petticoats and stood before him in all her corseted glory.

He is a pirate, she thought with a smirk.

But what if he really was just after the bounty? Her father had no doubt offered a reward for her return. How much, she didn't know. But given Sir Peter had sent twenty-thousand pounds with Woodcock in the event the *Molly* didn't catch up to the *Tuscan* before they reached Calais meant he did want her back.

That last comforting thought was replaced with a memory of what Blake had done to her earlier that evening. The pleasant frisson that shot through her body had her sighing, and she allowed sleep to take her.

In what seemed like only a moment later, she felt the pressure of a light kiss on her forehead. Opening her eyes, she was surprised to find the cabin lit from the sun.

"I really hate to wake you, my sweet, if only because I want nothing more than to climb in there and spend the entire day with you, but... we must be going."

Barbara blinked her eyes several times before Blake's face came into view. "Going?" she repeated. She sat up, surprised to find him dressed in the clothes of a gentleman—doeskin breeches, a white shirt and silk cravat, conservative waistcoat and topcoat. Although his black boots probably hadn't been made by Hoby, they were shined to a high gloss. "You're dressed. And not like a pirate."

The captain grinned. "You needn't sound so disappointed," he teased. Then he sobered. "Unless you are. In which case—"

"I'm only disappointed you did not spend the night with me," Barbara replied, pushing out her lower lip in a pout. Then she rolled her eyes. "I cannot believe how... how wanton I sounded just then."

Chuckling, Blake leaned over and kissed her. "If it helps, I do not mind. I do apologize for having left you alone. Duty and all," he said.

"Do you think me fast?" she asked in a whisper.

He frowned. "No. I..." He paused, wondering if she had changed her mind about their plans for the future. "I hadn't given it any thought, in fact. Other than I hope you're only fast with me," he added then.

"If there's another pirate in line for your heart, then I need to know now so I can challenge him to a duel."

Barbara giggled. "There is not."

Blake angled his head, happy to see her humored. "We docked a few minutes ago. I've sent a caddy to secure a hackney for us, and I've brought breakfast for you." He didn't add that another courier had been sent with a brief summary of what had happened to the Foreign Office. Blake knew Lord Chamberlain would be chafed if he wasn't kept apprised of the situation, and besides, an aristocrat would have to oversee the arrest of a baron.

Immune from regular prosecution, Lord Dorchester would have to be found guilty by his fellow lords in Parliament in order to suffer any punishment for his crime.

Blinking again, Barbara slowly sat up and allowed her legs to dangle from the edge of the bed. "Oh, bless you," she murmured, her stomach growling so it was almost audible. She winced when she remembered her hair probably looked worse than a rat's nest. "I don't suppose you could do anything with my hair?" she half-asked as she stood and moved to shake out her gown and petticoats. "I'm helpless without a looking glass and comb." Blake had hung her garments over the back of a chair, so they weren't as wrinkled as when they had come out of the valise the day before.

He grinned. "Let's get you dressed first, and while you have something to eat, I'll see what I can do."

Given his somewhat impatient manner, Barbara wondered if he was insisting she get dressed because he was now seeing her by the light of day and had decided he didn't like what he saw. She was about to ask when Blake said, "Truth be told, I'd really rather you not get dressed, because I admit to enjoying this version of you in the daylight."

"Oh," she managed, feeling immense relief. She stood on tip-toes and kissed him full on the mouth.

Blake hugged her hard and then pushed her away from his body. "Now you really must stop tempting me," he murmured. "Or I shall ruin you and tell your father I couldn't help myself." He could just imagine having to meet the man on a foggy morning in Wimbledon Common, holding a dueling pistol while Nelson stood nearby and watched his captain succumb to a bullet.

Barbara paused before she pulled on her petticoats without his assistance, thinking she rather liked tempting him. Who would have ever thought her a temptress? But when it was time to pull on the coral gown, she allowed him to hold it open as she stepped into it. She felt his deft fingers close the buttons up her back, and she grinned when he placed a kiss at the nape of her neck.

"'Tis a beautiful color on you," he whispered.

A shiver raced down her spine, and it was everything Barbara could do to keep quiet. She wanted to beg him to undress her. Return her to the bed. Ravish her.

Perhaps she could do that on their wedding day.

He led her to his small desk, where a covered tray lay atop pages of maps and charts. When she was seated, she removed the cover to find a plate of coddled eggs, toast, and a rasher of bacon. A cup of tea completed the breakfast. "This looks good," she murmured as she helped herself to a fork and tucked into the meal.

Blake pulled a comb from his kit, and starting at the bottom of her hair, began to work out the brown snarls. "Unlike most pirate ships, we have an actual cook on board," he replied.

"I thought you said this wasn't a pirate ship."

"We are not one on this day, it's true," he acknowledged. "Maybe tomorrow, though."

Barbara gave a start. "Why tomorrow?"

Blake paused in his task, trying to decide how much he could tell her. "We... have a mission. One that was supposed to have started yesterday," he explained. "There's something else you should know."

"Oh?"

"The *Tuscan* followed us into port." Although the other ship could have overtaken them somewhere near Walmer Castle, the smaller vessel had instead kept abreast of the *Molly*. Shortly after sunrise and above the sound of the sluicing water around their hulls, Captain Bimmington had shouted the information that had him ordering the *Tuscan* to turn around and return to London. Althea Woodcock was standing next to him as he did so, fear etched on her tear-stained face.

Her eyes widening in surprise, Barbara turned to look up at him. "Woodcock?" she questioned.

Blake nodded. "Seems there's more to your kidnapping than we thought," he replied, slowly drawing the comb through her long hair. During the ball, her hair had been pinned up into a mass of curls atop her head. Now it fell in golden waves to just past her shoulders. He drew a hand over the soft silk, smoothing it down as he drew the comb through it with his other hand. "Your hair is like liquid gold," he murmured. He pressed his nose onto the crown of her head and inhaled. "And it smells like lemon."

Barbara set down her fork, reveling in the quiet moment. "You're making an excellent lady's maid. I don't miss Woodcock one bit."

Thinking he might share what he had learned

from the woman earlier that morning, Blake dipped his head. "I fear Woodcock may have been misunderstood in all of this."

Turning to look up at him, Barbara's brows furrowed. "Whatever do you mean? She tried to steal…"

A pounding at the door had Blake hurrying to open it.

"Hackney's here, as is the Runner you sent for," Nelson said in a quiet voice. "What do we do with the baron? He's howlin' mad, complainin' to whoever goes near the brig and wonderin' as to the whereabouts of the lady's maid."

"Then don't let anyone go near him. Leave him in the brig for now. I'll let Chamberlain decide his fate," Blake said. "Is Miss Woodcock secure?"

"Indeed. She's done nothin' but weep the whole time she's been aboard. But she's scare't of him. Says he'll kill her if he can get his hands on her."

Blake sighed. "We'll take her with us in the hackney. Let Chamberlain decide what's next." He turned to Barbara, who had joined him at the door. "Are you ready to go?"

She glanced between Nelson and Blake. "I just have to pack a few things." Hurrying to her valise, she shoved the costume and petticoats into it and took a quick look around. Spotting a small looking glass over the pitcher and ewer, she paused to look at herself.

She was prepared for worse than the reflection she saw. Sure she would have suffered a sunburn from her time on deck the day before, she was surprised to find her skin appeared only lightly golden, and it seemed to glow from within. Although she would have preferred to pull her hair up into a bun, she had no pins to secure it. Seeing how the waves curled at her collarbones had a slight grin touching her lips. Even though she still didn't think she was especially fetching, she wasn't ugly. And perhaps her wide-set eyes gave her an exotic air.

A thought of what Blake had done to her the night before had her grin lifting her cheeks, and her eyes brightened with the memory. "I'm ready," she announced, grabbing the valise as she passed the bed.

Blake took the valise from her and led her to the ramp. Several crewmen paused to bow in her direction as she passed by, and she dipped a curtsy in return. "Thank you all for rescuing me," she called out as Blake offered his arm.

Barbara placed a hand on it, a sense of melancholy settling over her. Although she hadn't enjoyed a single moment aboard the *Tuscan*, she had felt comfortable on the *Molly*. Safe.

Shouts and whistles brought her out of her

reverie. She marveled at the bustle of activity that surrounded the ship and the one moored further down the dock. Porters pulled carts filled with cargo while the unmistakeable odors of seawater and wet wood and sweat filled her nostrils. She couldn't possibly see everything, but she did recognize Captain Bimmington. He was making his way in their direction.

"Begging your pardon, Miss Wycliff, but I wanted to apologize for what happened," he said as he removed his tricorn and gave her a deep bow. "Had I known who you really were and that you had been kidnapped, I assure you, I would have sent word to the authorities when Mr. Smith brought you on board."

Barbara acknowledged his apology with a nod. "Thank you, Captain. I'm sure my father will take that into consideration."

Bimmington blinked, and Blake turned to stare down at her. "Consideration?" the two men repeated.

She allowed a slight shrug. "Sir Peter is looking to buy some merchant ships, and I believe the *Tuscan* is one of them. Good day, sir." She curtsied and made her way in the direction of the hackney.

Blake hurried to catch up. "You didn't tell me your father was going to buy the *Tuscan*," he said, as he opened the door to the hackney.

"Nor did I say that he was," she replied, her comment followed by a shrug.

"You minx," he accused in a whisper filled with humor. Poor Bimmington probably thought he would be out of a position soon.

CHAPTER 16
HOMECOMING

A few minutes later Blake helped Barbara into the equipage knowing Miss Woodcock was already in it. Pressed into one corner, her hands tied behind her back and a valise on the bench next to her, Althea looked as if she had lost her best friend.

Perhaps she had.

"Woodcock," Barbara said as she took the seat opposite the lady's maid. She pretended indifference towards the servant, not yet sure what to believe about the woman.

Althea nodded in her direction, sniffling before she said, "My lady."

Outside, Barbara could hear Blake giving the driver instructions, and then he joined them, settling onto the bench next to her. "We've a ways to go to get to Parkenhurst House," he murmured. "If you'd like to sleep, I'm happy to provide a shoulder."

Barbara knew she would have accepted his offer if they had been the only ones in the hackney, but with Woodcock's presence, she decided she'd best behave. She still had no idea what to believe when it came to the lady's maid's involvement in what had happened. "I rather doubt I'll be able to sleep." She sighed. "Has word been sent to my father?"

"The courier I sent to Horseguards was to make his way to Parkenhurst House next. Depending on the morning's traffic, your father may learn you are on your way home before we even arrive."

"Thank you," she replied.

The hackney clattered along the streets of London, and Barbara watched as familiar landmarks appeared beyond the windows. The Tower. St. Paul's. Lincolns Inn Fields. Covent Gardens. Odd that she had barely given them a glance the last time she had seen them.

When the hackney finally came to a halt in front of Parkenhurst House, she jerked awake, her head having settled against Blake's arm sometime before they reached Mayfair.

Blake stepped down and offered his hand. Once Barbara was out, he waved for Althea to follow. Reluctantly, she slid across the bench. With her hands behind her back, she had no choice but to allow him to help her down. Then he lifted her valise from the bench, hefting it to determine if the items Nelson had packed into it were still in there.

But it felt empty.

He was about to ask her when she had discovered the substitution, but the front door to the Palladian mansion opened even before they made it to the wrought iron fence that lined the front of the property.

Four stories tall and landscaped with topiary trees, perfectly manicured boxwoods, and rows of flowers, it was apparent Parkenhurst belonged to a wealthy man. "Welcome home, Miss Wycliff," the butler said with a toothy grin as he stepped aside.

"Thank you, Broadus. Is my father at home?"

"Of course. He hasn't left here since word of your kidnapping," the butler replied, his attention shifting to the lady's maid. He frowned when he saw that her hands were tied behind her back. "He's in the study."

But he wasn't. Sir Peter was already making his way in their direction. "Barbara? *Barbara!*" He doubled his steps as his daughter hurried to meet him halfway. "Are you all right?" he asked as he pulled her into a brief hug. "We've been worried sick."

"I am, Father. Thanks to Captain Russell," she said, as she turned to wave in Blake's direction. "His ship caught up to the *Tuscan* before it made it to Calais, and he carried me over wooden planks onto his ship, and his men captured Lord Dorchester—"

"Dorchester?" Sir Peter repeated in alarm. He turned to Blake just as the captain joined them. "Captain Russell, I presume?"

"I am," Blake said as he offered a nod. Valises dangled from both of his hands. "From your reaction, I suppose you've not yet heard word from Lord Chamberlain."

The baronet shook his head. "I haven't. Spent most of the night before last over at Chamberlain House, though, once Woodcock told us what had happened." He gave Blake a thorough inspection, apparently liking what he saw when he gave an assessing nod. "From what my daughter just told me, I take it you captained the ship that was sent to chase down the *Tuscan*?"

"Indeed. It was my pleasure, though," Blake replied. "I actually met your daughter at Lord Weatherstone's masked ball the night of the kidnapping."

Sir Peter seemed to think on this bit of information before he led them to his study, calling out instructions to his butler as he did so. At the last moment, he turned and directed his attention on Althea Woodcock. "Why is she bound like that?"

"She's a suspect, sir," Blake replied. "Seems she was working for Dorchester."

The baronet gave a shake of his head. He glanced down at the valises and then back up to Blake. "And what are these?

"The ransom money," Blake replied as he lifted the heavy one.

Sir Peter gave a start and then shook his head. "But, I didn't send any ransom money. Chamberlain told me not to."

Blake blinked.

Barbara blinked.

And all three of them turned to regard Althea with expectant expressions. She stood just beyond the vestibule, her head lifting when she realized she was the subject of their attention.

Behind her, the butler moved to open the door, and a breathless Matthew Fitzsimmons, Viscount Chamberlain, entered just as Woodcock said, "I had to take the money, or he would have killed her. He told me so during the ball," she wailed.

"Who?" Lord Chamberlain demanded.

Althea gave a start and whirled around to find the head of the Foreign Office regarding her with suspicion.

"Lord Dorchester," she replied. "He kidnapped my mistress. Told me he was going to take her to

France. Demand a ransom. And that if he didn't get twenty-thousand pounds for her, he was going to kill her." The words tumbled out as tears once again fell onto her cheeks. "So I stuffed the money into my mistress' valise and took it with me when I delivered the note to Captain Russell. I wasn't stealin' it. I promise."

"I asked you point blank if you had the ransom money, and you said you didn't," Blake reminded her.

She rolled her eyes. "I wasn't about to admit I had twenty-thousand pounds with me."

"Why ever not?"

"You're a pirate," she replied. "I saw the skull and crossbones flying over your ship."

Blake rolled his eyes, deciding she had a point.

"Why did you board the *Tuscan* after I was rescued?" Barbara countered, her hands going to her hips.

Blake's attention was captured by her bosom, thrust out such as it was as Barbara conveyed her mistrust of the lady's maid's comment. He was about to say something based on what Nelson had told him, but Althea did instead.

"I had to get away from Dorchester," she cried. "He would have killed me to get to the money."

"Russell, why are her hands tied?" Chamberlain queried.

"Because we think she was working with Dorchester to fleece Sir Peter out of twenty-thousand pounds," Blake explained. "She used to be a maid in the baron's household. Then she was hired here as Miss Wycliff's lady's maid under suspicious circumstances."

"But, I provided a character," Althea argued. "I had to get out of his house. He's a repugnant—"

"You were smiling at him during your dance with him at the ball," Barbara claimed, her hands still on her hips, almost as if she knew she had Blake's full attention. She directed a grin in his direction, and he winked at her.

"I was *acting*," Althea countered. "I had to pretend I was going to help him."

"Or what?" Chamberlain challenged.

Althea grimaced. "He would have spread lies about me. About my family. Made sure I couldn't get hired anywhere."

Chamberlain turned to the butler, who had just joined them in the hall carrying a tea tray. "Were you involved with Miss Woodcock's hiring?"

Broadus's brows lifted in surprise. "Yes," he answered, although reluctantly.

"Was there a particular reason you hired *her?*"

The butler's head seemed to shrink into his shoulders. "No one else applied."

Chamberlain seemed about to ask another question of the butler, but instead turned his attention onto Althea. "Where did you get the twenty-thousand pounds?"

Sir Peter cleared his throat. "I was about to ask the same question, but now I think I may know," he said, once again waving them into his study. He made his way to his desk, searched for a key in one drawer, and then unlocked one of the bottom drawers. "I'll be damned," he murmured.

Blake lifted the heavier valise onto the desk. "Are you missing twenty-thousand pounds, perhaps?"

Sir Peter opened the valise and stared inside. "Is this some sort of joke?"

Frowning, Blake did the same and then gave a quelling glance. "That's your daughter's Little Bo Beep gown," he said. "Made for a rather fetching costume, but poor Miss Wycliff was forced to wear it until just last night when we discovered the gown she's wearing now was inside the valise," he explained as he waved to Barbara's frock. "My first mate managed to switch valises on Woodcock, so your daughter could have a change of clothes as well as get the ransom money back."

He set the empty valise on the floor and then pulled the pink satin gown from the full valise followed by the three petticoats and the set of drawers, settling each item over an arm until only the money was left at the bottom of the bag.

"Good God!" Sir Peter whispered, his attention going to Althea. She stood next to Chamberlain, who had a grip on one of her arms.

"He made me do it. If I hadn't, he would have killed me, too," she said in a plaintive voice.

"How did you even know about the money in the first place?" Blake asked, the memory of something she had said the day before niggling at the back of his brain.

Althea dipped her head. "Sir Peter spoke of it in my hearing. Said he never knew if—"

"If I might be in need of blunt in a hurry," Sir Peter finished for her. He huffed before turning his attention to Lord Chamberlain. "I thought you said you had a man following Dorchester," he said, obviously annoyed to learn it was Dorchester who had kidnapped his daughter.

"That was me," Blake acknowledged, lifting a hand. "Dorchester gave me the slip during the supper, though. Rather than return to the ballroom by the main doors, he exited through another set of doors into a hallway, and by the time I sorted he had left the mansion, his coach was speeding off, as was yours," he explained. "I wrongly assumed Miss Wycliff was in your coach. I didn't even know

Dorchester was in possession of your daughter until I received word from Lord Chamberlain the following morning. Had I any idea, I assure you, I would have pursued his coach."

Sir Peter nodded his understanding, and then his attention turned to his daughter, his graying brows furrowing. "Did he ruin you?"

Barbara shook her head. She explained what had happened up until Blake carried her to the *Molly*, including how the *Tuscan's* captain didn't believe her claim that she was kidnapped.

"So, where is Dorchester now? I've a mind to maim that man," Sir Peter claimed.

"In the brig of my ship. I thought it best he remain there, seeing as how he cannot be arrested," Blake answered in disgust.

"Whatever do you mean? He kidnapped my daughter!"

"He's a baron. A lord. He's protected from civil law," Blake replied.

"But not from his peers," Chamberlain stated. "Russell, I received your missive and sent a couple of my men to retrieve the bastard. He'll be held until the lord chancellor can be summoned."

"Will he be sent to Newgate?" Blake asked, worried for Barbara's safety. He moved to stand next to her, gratified when she placed a hand on his arm.

"That would be preferable," Chamberlain replied, just before his brows furrowed. "You seem especially concerned."

Blake glanced over at Barbara. Still holding the dress and petticoats over one arm, he looked like a valet assigned to the wrong sex. "I am concerned. For Miss Wycliff. Dorchester will seek revenge against her should he ever have the opportunity to do so," he said. "I must be assured of her safety."

"Oh?" Sir Peter put in. "I think that was supposed to be my line."

"Well, yes. And it would have been if she hadn't agreed to marry me," Blake replied. "That is, if you're of a mind to give me permission to court her," he went on, grimacing when he realized this wasn't the way he planned to do it. "I'm in love with her, you see." He furrowed his brows. "I think I have been since I danced with her at the ball."

Chamberlain blinked.

Sir Peter blinked.

Althea allowed a watery grin. "How romantic," she wailed.

"Barbara?" Sir Peter said as he turned his attention on her. "Would you care to explain?"

She glanced up at Blake before she said, "We spoke at the ball. He was dressed as a pirate. We danced twice—he taught me how to waltz. And then the next time I saw him, he was on the deck of the *Molly* shouting he was there to rescue me."

"I was a bit dramatic," Blake murmured, his face taking on a dark red shade.

"And he waved his sword about—"

"Cutlass, my sweet."

"His cutlass about to ensure no one on the *Tuscan* challenged him. One of the crewmen even knocked Mr. Smith—"

"That was Fitz, our sailing master," Blake said, for Chamberlain's benefit.

"Who is Mr. Smith?" Chamberlain queried, his brows furrowing in confusion.

"Lord Dorchester. He used the name Mr. Smith when he arranged transportation to Calais," Blake explained.

Barbara took a breath. "So Mr. Fitz knocked out Lord Dorchester just as Blake lifted me into his arms and carried me to the *Molly*." She sighed as a grin appeared to brighten her face. "It was exciting and frightening and awful, because I was still in that hideous Bo Peep costume—"

"It's not hideous," Blake interrupted. "It's rather fetching on you." When he noted her quelling glance, he added, "But I like this one better."

"How romantic," Althea murmured again.

Sir Peter furrowed a brow. "So... once you were

on the *Molly?* What happened?" he asked, suspicion evident in his voice.

"Well, we realized Woodcock was on the *Tuscan,*" she replied. "But Nelson—he's the first mate—he had switched the valises so that my valise, with the money and this gown, was still on the *Molly*. So I was finally able to rid myself of that awful costume and get some sleep since Blake allowed me the use of his quarters for the rest of the trip back to London." She beamed in delight as she stared up at Blake.

He grinned back at her and dropped a kiss on the crown of her head.

"Did *you* ruin her?" Sir Peter asked in alarm.

Blake's eyes widened. "Why, no sir. But I do wish to court your daughter—"

"What about the *Molly?*" Chamberlain asked, with just as much alarm.

"Oh, I can still captain a ship," he replied. "Continue my work for you," he added, realizing he couldn't admit he worked for the Foreign Service. "We talked about this, and Miss Wycliff is agreeable to the idea."

Sir Peter cleared his throat. "She might be, but... are you just doing this for her dowry?"

"Father!"

Blake frowned. "No, sir. I'm quite able to support a wife on my income," he replied. "However, there is the matter of pay for my crew's help in retrieving your daughter."

It was Chamberlain's turn to clear his throat. "Sir Peter, if you recall your words from a few nights ago? In my orders to Captain Russell, I implied that there was a reward involved in Miss Wycliff's safe return."

"Oh, yes, of course," Sir Peter replied. He glanced down at the valise. "Is twenty-thousand pounds sufficient?" he asked. He pushed the valise in Blake's direction.

Blake and Chamberlain exchanged glances. "Split fifteen ways means over thirteen hundred pounds a piece," Blake whispered. "I may never get them back on board."

Sir Peter angled his head to one side. "You would do that?"

Blake gave a shake of his head. "Do what, sir?"

"Split the money evenly with your crew?"

Blake lifted a shoulder. "Of course. All the members of my crew receive an equal share of any reward. Any bounty," he replied.

"How long have you been a ship's captain?" Sir Peter asked, his manner having changed to open curiosity.

"A year now. I was the first mate of the *Molly* before that."

"Ever been interested in captaining a merchant ship?" the baronet asked with an arched brow.

Dipping his head, Blake dared a glance at Barbara before he said, "I hadn't given it any thought."

"I'm considering the purchase of a fleet of ships," Sir Peter explained. "Wilson's fleet."

"Now, see here, sir. You cannot be taking my best captain," Chamberlain argued.

"I think that should be up to my future son-in-law, don't you?" Sir Peter replied.

Blake inhaled slowly as Barbara tightened her hold on his arm. "I told you," she whispered.

Turning to Chamberlain, Blake said, "It's all right. Nelson is ready to take command, and Fitz would make an excellent first mate. He's all about the rules."

The viscount huffed. "So, how are you going to split the reward?"

"He keeps ten-thousand pounds as my daughter's dowry, and the rest can be split fourteen ways," Sir Peter announced.

Chamberlain furrowed a brow, as if he was attempting to do the math in his head.

"Seven-hundred, fourteen pounds and ten shillings," Blake whispered.

"You have a mission to complete regarding a certain French smuggler," Chamberlain whispered, a reminder of the mission they had been about to embark on when they received the note about the kidnapping.

"So I won't distribute the reward until we're in the Channel," Blake reasoned.

"Agreed," the viscount said with a nod. He turned to the baronet. "Well, good day. Perhaps I'll see you at White's tonight?"

Sir Peter shook his head. "Maybe tomorrow. I shall spend this evening having dinner with my daughter. Seems she won't be around much longer, and I rather imagine she'll be planning a wedding here shortly."

Barbara beamed in delight.

"What about Miss Woodcock?" Blake asked, his attention back on the viscount.

Chamberlain gave the lady's maid a quelling glance. "If she cooperates and testifies against Dorchester, then I think we'll forego any charges against her," he reasoned.

Althea's eyes widened. "I will, of course, as long as the baron is kept locked up," she replied.

"Perhaps you might consider a move to the country. Maybe take a position in a manor house?" Chamberlain hinted. "I rather doubt Dorchester would bother trying to find you even if he wasn't locked up in Newgate." He moved to untie her hands.

"We'll see to a character for you," Sir Peter

offered. "And pay for the past month. Broadus will escort you to your room, and you can pack up your things." He glanced down at the empty valise near his feet. "You can use this," he offered, lifting the bag and offering it to her.

"Thank you, sir," she said as she rubbed her wrists and then took the valise. She left the study with Broadus.

"Well, it seems I'll be heading out in the morning," Blake said as he turned his attention to Barbara. "Low tide. Perhaps you would agree to a walk in the park? Maybe an ice at Gunther's?"

Barbara grinned. "I'd like that." She turned to her father, intending to ask if she could go, but he merely waved a hand.

"Go on," he said with a sigh. "But have her back before dinner," he warned. "Or I'll report that she's been kidnapped."

"Very good, sir," Blake said as he gave a bow. He took the valise in one hand and offered the other to Barbara.

When they headed up the stairs, Barbara gave him a sideways glance. "Are we really going to the park?" she asked in a whisper.

Blake blinked. "Did you... wish to go somewhere else?"

She gave him a quelling glance. "Remember what you said? About when we were betrothed?"

His brows furrowed in confusion before he realized what she meant. "Today?" he asked in surprise.

"You think me fast," she said on a sigh.

"No, that's not it. I just... I didn't think you would want to lose your virtue on your first day back. Given what's happened and all."

She stopped in front of her bedchamber and pushed open the door to reveal an ornately decorated room in peaches and greens. "I've thought of almost nothing else since last night," she murmured. "Especially since I didn't do anything for you."

Blake paused on the threshold, his gaze taking in the gilded plasterwork and rich fabrics. "That's not true," he murmured as he finally crossed into the bedchamber and then quickly shut the door. "It gave me a great deal of pleasure to be able to see to yours," he argued. "Besides, I really don't think it's wise for us to do it here."

"Why ever not? The bed is comfortable—"

"Everyone in the household will hear," he argued.

Her eyes widened. "They will?"

He rolled his own eyes. "My sweet, when I make love to you, I intend to have you screaming with pleasure for the entire world to hear," he claimed. "Or, at least so it can be heard in the next door apartment."

"Apartment?" she repeated.

"I have one in Picadilly."

"We'll go there, then."

Blake allowed a chuckle before he kissed her thoroughly. "I do hope you're always this willing," he murmured.

"Threaten me with your sword, and I will be."

"Cutlass, you mean."

She shook her head. "Sword," she corrected, her hand cupping his hardened manhood through the placket of his breeches.

"I stand corrected," he replied happily.

EPILOGUE

A few months later

Barbara awoke to the gentle sway of her father's newest acquisition. The *Barbara*, captained by her husband and manned by a crew of fourteen, was due to make its maiden voyage to Belgium later that morning. Although the hold wasn't full, it would be on the return trip, arrangements having been made for them to pick up a shipment bound for London.

The bed in which she had been sleeping for the past few nights was proving far too comfortable, but then it helped that her companion was seeing to her comfort in more ways than one.

"Good morning, sleepy head," Blake said, just before he kissed her forehead. "How is my treasure on this fine day?"

She grinned and returned the kiss. "I don't know

why I'm so tired of late," she whispered, delighting in the feel of his warm hands as they smoothed over her night rail in their quest to awaken other parts of her body.

Blake lifted the fabric of her gown until her belly was exposed. "I've no idea, either," he lied, struggling to keep from chuckling. At some point, she would realize she hadn't had her monthly courses the entire time they'd been married. Until then, he intended to simply revel in having her all to himself. Once the babe was born, he would have to share.

At least, that's what Nelson had told him. How the new captain of the *Molly* could know such a thing, he didn't dare guess, but thought it was best to be prepared.

As for the new captain's other announcement, Blake found he wasn't a bit surprised. Althea Woodcock and Nelson had said their vows a few days after the *Molly's* return from their mission to capture the French privateer.

Apparently Nelson had decided the former lady's maid was fruitful enough for him. Either that, or Althea had threatened to divulge secrets from their past.

Blake kissed Barbara's belly and then was about to move farther down when he remembered news he learned the night before. "I received a missive from

Viscount Chamberlain," he said between kisses on her thighs.

"Oh?"

"Seems Dorchester's fate has been decided." He regretted having said anything when she suddenly sat up and the target his tongue intended to touch disappeared.

"Newgate?" she guessed. Her eyes widened. "Or will he dance the hempen jig?"

His brows rising at hearing her mention the pirate term for a hanging, Blake shook his head. "Australia. He's being transported tomorrow," Blake murmured, his hands gripping her hips in an effort to reposition her.

"Is that good?"

"It is," he replied, settling his head between her thighs once she had her knees bent. "He'll never be able to threaten you—or Woodcock—again." The cur had certainly tried, but any letters he wrote were intercepted before they could make their way to the intended recipients.

"Now, I'm going after buried treasure," he warned.

Blake delighted in hearing Barbara's inhalation of breath as his tongue circled its target. Having several months of experience in the matter, he knew exactly what to do to have her crying out his name followed by a series of platitudes and words of gratitude.

This morning was no different.

His favorite moment was always the next one, when she begged for him. That she sometimes did so at other times—rather inconvenient times—meant his crew had quickly learned he was at her beck and call.

At the threat of docked pay, they were good about not mentioning how he was being led by his cock by his new wife.

And anyway, he didn't mind.

"I need your sword," she whispered, breathless. "Please."

And there it was.

"Prepare to be boarded," he warned with a grin, just before he impaled her, groaning as he shoved his sword in her warm, wet sheath.

He loved how her torso lifted from the bed, her breasts bobbing about as he thrust into her over and over. How her thighs gripped his sides so his hands could cup the sides of her breasts and his thumbs could tease her engorged nipples.

What better bounty could there be?

Ecstasy, of course. He knew when it claimed her, for he could feel her inner muscles clenching on him, pulling his sword deeper into her. When he allowed his own ecstasy only a moment later, he was swept into a maelstrom of sensation so pleasurable, he often wondered how he would make his way back to the surface.

He always did. Inhaling deeply and reveling in the shivers set off by fingernails scraping his scalp, he sought refuge on her body, a life raft on which he floated until he was finally forced to either get up for the day or roll over and sleep at night.

At the moment, he couldn't quite decide which he should do.

Such was the pleasure of a pirate.

ABOUT THE AUTHOR

A self-described nerd and student of history, Linda Rae spent many years as a published technical writer specializing in 3D graphics workstations, software and 3D animation (her movie credits include SHREK and SHREK 2). Getting lost in the rabbit holes of research has resulted in historical romances set in the Regency-era as well as Ancient Greece.

A fan of action-adventure movies, she can frequently be found at the local cinema. Although she no longer has any tropical fish, she follows the San Jose Sharks and makes her home in Cody, Wyoming.

For more information:
www.lindaraesande.com
Sign up for Linda Rae's newsletter:
Regency Romance with a Twist
Follow Linda Rae's blog:
Regency Romance with a Twist